GW00691501

The Danieli Conspiracy

Stone Lodge Publications Ltd.

Copyright © Stone Lodge Publications Ltd., 2005

Terry McCartney and John Doherty have asserted their right to be identified as the authors of this work under the Copyright, Designs and Patents Act, 1988

First published in the UK in 2005 by
Stone Lodge Publications Ltd.,
Stone Lodge, Ballycastle,
Northern Ireland BT54 6DJ

ISBN 0-9549851-0-9

Typeset in 11.5 Baskerville by Guildhall Press Ltd., Derry
Cover design by John McCandless
Printed and bound in Dublin by ColourBooks

In this work of fiction, the characters, places and events are either the product of the author's imagination or they are entirely fictitious. Any similarity between a character or characters in this work and an actual person or persons is entirely co-incidental and is not intended.

This book is sold subject to the condition that it shall not, by way of trade or otherwise, be lent, re-sold, hired out or otherwise circulated in any form of binding or cover other than that in which it is published and without a similar condition including this condition being imposed on the subsequent purchaser.

For Eleanor, Nola and John

ACKNOWLEDGEMENTS

I would like to thank the following people who have had to endure my telling of this story for 10 years. The Gandelli Family, my wife Eleanor, my daughter Nola and son John, my reliable and loyal colleague Jean Linton. Thanks also to the owners of the majestic Hotel Danieli, The Starwood Hotel Group in New York, and the crew of the yacht 'Genesis of Ballycastle' for their encouragement in chapter writing on the high seas,

Terry McCartney

I would like to express appreciation to the following people, without whose assistance 'The Danieli Conspiracy' would not have been possible: my wife Ann Tyre, my children Elinor, Grace, and Caolán, Lily Tyre, my friends Isadore and Sophie Ryan for their unfailing support and help with all matters Italian, my old friend Sara Tolchin, my oldest friends Christoph, Ursula and Anastasia Beck, cover designer John McCandless, Derry historian Richard Doherty, our lawyer Ted Harding, and my fellow journalists Breandán Delap, Richard Newell and Tony Hay,

John Doherty

1

Port of Londonderry, Northern Ireland, May 1942

"The Port of Londonderry has a total of 79 frigates, corvettes and destroyers in port this week, from the USA, Britain, and Sweden." The cheery voice of the newsreader on the American Forces Network rang through the lounge of Mulhern's Grand Central Bar.

Mary Black would probably pull a pint of porter for a man from every ship, before the night was out.

Five American sailors were lined on the barstools before her. Their boyish appearance, fresh-faced and crew-cut, was at odds with their rowdy, rough-necked conversation.

Since the US Naval Base had opened a year before, the city had become a melting pot of nationalities, a hub for ships from the American, Canadian, British, and Scandinavian fleets. Derry was the port of anchor for the 'Londonderry Ferry', the destroyer escorts that accompanied cargo ships into the no-man's-land of the mid-Atlantic.

Under the stained glass frontage that looked out on to the Strand Road, a group of British sailors, fresh from a month at sea, were making up for lost time. The beer was flowing. Not a woman in the city was safe.

Mary Black watched them through the thick cloud that floated like London smog above the room. There had been three brawls between British and Yanks in the last week. She hoped there would be no trouble tonight.

"Five more pints of this fine beer, ma'am," said the American at the end of the group of five at the bar. The others laughed at his mock admiration. The malty, ruby-red Irish ale was so unlike the lighter beer back home.

"And ma'am, may I have the privilege of knowing your name, since we'll be seeing so much of each other in the next five days?"

"It's Mary Black. And less of the sweet-talk out of you. I know how charming you Yanks are, with your chewing gum and your ice-cream, and I know what you're after, too."

"Miss Mary Black, you do me wrong." The American raised his hands in mock supplication.

"Twenty thousand sailors this week, and believe me ma'am, you are meeting the five charmingest, most sincerest, most nicest guys in town." He lifted his arm in a fussy flourish, as if removing a feathered cap from his head. The move smacked vaguely of Danny Kaye.

"May I introduce: Boilermaker, First Class, Walt Butzen from Fresno. Ships' Cook, 2nd Class, young Marty Marosky from New York. Radioman, 2nd Class, Tom 'The Moose' Pavlovski of Seattle Washington. Lastly, my good self, Delbert Telesco, from Cleveland Ohio. Engineman, First Class!".

A glass floated over his shoulder with an arm attached, followed by a smiling local face. "Gerry Devlin. Derryman, First Class. Pint, Mary, when you're ready."

The sailors laughed, and slapped the local on the back, as he turned to go back to his seat.

Mary Black placed the first of their frothing jars of beer on the counter. She turned to the radioman. "So. Why do they call you 'Moose'? You don't look so terrible to me."

Another peal of laughter went up from the group. Telesco dived in, before the Moose could answer. "Hell, ma'am, it's because he can't take a walk without getting himself shot." The uproar grew louder than before.

"When the Japs came in to Pearl Harbor, Moose was off-duty, fishing from the rocks. He still took a bullet in the butt. Hell, he even kept the shorts with the hole to prove it!" said Telesco.

The Moose grinned and stared at the bar.

"C'mon Moose, show the lady your battle scars!"

Moose didn't need to be asked twice. This was his party piece. Glasses were lifted as he clambered on to the bar. To raucous yelping from the Americans, he propped his foot against the beertaps, dropped his chinos, and pulled down one side of the boxer shorts beneath. From the charity boxes at his feet, St. Martin and St. Anthony smiled beatifically upward at a red welt on his right buttock.

"There is some corner of a foreign butt that is forever Tokyo!" yelped Marosky.

Now, the Moose pulled back the other side of his shorts. The tattoo was a Stars and Stripes in patriotic red and blue. His buddies' enthusiasm reached fever pitch. Telesco whooped like an Indian brave. Butzen fisted the air like a bible-belt preacher. Marosky raised his pint to his temple, in a mock salute. All of them screamed 'Way to go, Moose', and hammered the bar with the flat of their hands.

Somewhere at the back, Gerry Devlin rolled his eyes, and muttered 'God bless America' into his pint of stout.

The Moose clambered down out of the smoke-cloud, and back on to solid ground.

The Americans settled down again, and order was restored. Telesco rubbed the laughter from his eyes with the back of his hand. From his breast pocket, he drew a pack of Chesterfields, deftly tapping it on the bar so that one cigarette emerged. "Tailormade, ma'am?"

"Or a tickler if you want, Miss," said the Moose, offering a thin roll-up from a pale green tin.

Mary knew that if she accepted the cigarette, Telesco would produce the chewing gum and then, if he thought he had a chance with her, at least the promise of a pair of nylons. It was a pantomime she'd seen before. It ran in Mulhern's every night of the week.

Couple of beers later, he'd be offering to put them on her himself.

"I don't," said Mary, hardly looking up as she wiped a green cheesecloth around a wet beer glass. Somewhere in this war she had dropped the 'thanks'. Polite refusals were lost on a wolfpack of sex-crazy Yanks.

She stepped a little closer to the beertaps, remembering the thin black line running up the backs of her legs. Fake seams drawn in eye-pencil were the next best thing to real stockings, in a wartime town.

A second later, a half-drunk pint of red ale arc'd perfectly out of the British corner and shattered on the bar. Marosky and the Moose raised their arms, more concerned for their beer-spattered jackets than themselves.

"Bleedin' Yanks. Yanks go home. Oversexed, overpaid – and over 'ere." It was the standard insult, delivered in broad Cockney and slurred like it had been stretched sideways.

The owner of the accent steadied himself against his guffawing comrades, and lurched into the crowd towards the Moose. The sight of a rear end that was a vet of Pearl Harbor had been more than his sensibilities could take.

Moose looked round, but the quick retort came from Marosky. "And you damn limeys? Underpaid, undersexed – and under Eisenhower!"

"I hear those guys stop in the middle of battle to drink a cup of tea," Telesco hooted. The Yanks swirled around on their stools, like five desperados in a Kansas saloon.

The Moose was not going to be second. He led off like a prize racehorse, closely followed by Butzen, raising a barstool above his head. As they approached the first, Telesco and Marosky were jostling for position behind.

Half a dozen British, some airborne pints of ale, three or four squealing women and the five paddling Americans milled together in the middle of the floor. The women were swept to the sidelines as pushes turned into punches, and half-smoked cigarettes flew to the right and left.

Somebody pulled the door open, and, under the direction of Mary and several other neutral Irish, the front end of the fight spilled into the street. A paunchy shipfitter from LaGrange, Illinois, too sober to participate, rowed in beside Mary to help, and the rest of the throng rolled forward like a departing train.

The brawl contracted to cross the threshold, then widened again in the street like a sprawling, many-legged animal. The stamping and shouting formed a sound as raw as a hopper spilling coal into a dump-truck.

Mary reached out and prised the door closed on the last angry back.

She straightened up in relief, catching her breath, and looked around the room. The floor was a pool of swilling liquid, soggy, half-smoked Chesterfields, and glittering shards of broken glass. A box of matches had emptied on the floor. Its contents were sopping around in a pool of beer like a miniature logjam on a slow-flowing river.

Behind the bar, the large mirror was a mass of silver triangles. A jagged epicentre marked where a chair-leg had found its target. The chair lay upended on the wooden trellis beneath.

The dozen remaining drinkers had climbed up on the seats and were gazing through the windows, their drinks clutched to their chests. One woman had got too close to the front line. She was crying, a hand held to her aching cheek.

Mary peered at the brawl outside over the frosted glass in the door. She had seen it all before.

Nothing told her it was a moment that would change her life.

*****

Chief Petty Officer Joe Gandelli didn't have to be turning the corner into Great James Street, just as the fight spilled out Mulhern's and directly into his path.

But that is where he was, and this was not a situation the US navy's best-known war hero could ignore.

He plunged into the crowd and, standing a good head and shoulders above most of them, shoved his arm between two wrestling soldiers closest to him. The fight had lost its focus, and he was prising two Americans apart, one white, the other black, fighting their own private race war.

"Ok guys, Shore Patrol's on the way. Let's cool it off," he called, the levelness of his voice setting it apart from the bellowing of the crowd.

"Hey doughboy – what gives?" shouted the white soldier, whirling round, his face contorted with rage. Seeing Gandelli, he immediately relaxed.

"Jeez, Joe, you almost caught one on the nose there, man," he said, lowering his arm.

Gandelli patted them both on the shoulder, and stepped out to the left.

"Hey – is that the Moose!" he called over the crowd. "Looks like you made it for the fight this time."

The Moose ran his fingers through his hair, and patted a scuffed cheekbone to check for blood. Finding none, he grinned broadly and walked to meet Gandelli, away from the dispersing melee.

"Gotta light, Joe?" The Moose flipped a cigarette on to his lower lip, and offered the pack. Gandelli lit him from a small silver lighter with a bird engraving on the lid. The British were moving on, and the rest of the Yanks were already standing in ones and twos as the crowd calmed in the cool air.

The show was over, and in the bar, heads began to disappear from the windows. Only Mary Black continued to stare at the sailor who had broken up the fight. Her breath misted the polished glass.

*****

At eleven thirty the next morning, the velvet voice of Dinah Shore was floating out of the pub radio as Mary Black swept up the last fragments of glass from the damp carpet.

"I'll be seeing you in all the old familiar places

That this heart of mine embraces..."

She hummed absentmindedly with the music, but paid no attention to the heart-rending lyric. At 22, a melancholy ballad had little bearing on her life. Romance, she thought, like all the great adventures, was ahead of her yet.

A telephone call had announced that the US Navy Assessor would call at 11 o'clock, to inspect the pub and settle for damages caused. She was concerned to replace the mirror; beyond that, Mulhern's had lost only a few glasses and a lot of warm beer. Maybe they might stretch to cleaning the carpet, and perhaps replace a couple of broken barstools, she thought.

Through the frosted glass, Mary saw the angular outline of the green jeep draw up, and three figures alighted. The door of the pub was open. Joe Gandelli hopped lightly up on to the doorstep and craned his neck to see into the farthest corners of the room.

"Hi ma'am, we've just come to take a look around, make sure you don't have to carry the can for all this," he said. Behind him, the Assessor entered clutching a clipboard, followed by a thin-faced sailor with a rifle, who looked all of sixteen years old.

"We sure are sorry about the trouble last night. We have disciplined the men responsible, and we're gonna make it right up to you ma'am," said the Assessor. His drone indicated that this was his set speech for such occasions. He pushed between the tables and sat down, folding back the top page on the clipboard and pulling a pen from his breast pocket. He looked at Mary with a world-weary smile.

Gandelli sat down with them at the table. The young guard stood to attention by the door. "If we can agree with you now, ma'am, I see no reason why we can't get you paid by tomorrow morning," said the Assessor.

Mary ran through the damages, and the Assessor fluently took notes. "I'd say it would take £130 to cover it – that would clean the carpet, too" she concluded.

"I would have no problem with that figure, ma'am," the Assessor responded, smiling. At this point, Gandelli leaned over, and whispered something in his ear.

"In fact, let's say £150, to include a *new* carpet," the Assessor pronounced. Vigorously, he ripped a chit from his notepad, and folded it into an envelope.

"Now, that takes care of that. Joe, I also gotta get to the Harvest Ballroom uptown," said the Assessor. The Harvest was the toughest venue in Derry, and the Navy Assessor was a weekly visitor.

"You carry on up there with Sam and the jeep, Captain. If you don't mind. That way, me and the kid can help Miss Black finish her tidy-up," said Gandelli.

"I'll call again in the morning, ma'am. Thank you for your time," said the Assessor, and went out to join his driver. The young sailor placed his weapon behind the bar, and, hunkering down below table level, began lifting glass from under seats and in carpet nooks.

The Assessor was hardly out of sight, when the door opened again. It was the Moose.

Joe set to tying up the coal sack Mary had filled with assorted debris.

"Mr. Gandelli, be careful, that's full of glass."

"I'll just get it outside, Miss Black, and we'll take it away for you in the jeep, when the Captain gets back."

Joe called the young sailor to his aid and the pair set off, lugging the sack out the door to drag it to the street corner. The Moose and Mary were alone in the bar. He was ill-at-ease, gnawing insistently on a wad of chewing gum.

"Ma'am, I wanted to apologise to you personally 'bout last night. Me showin' my war wound set the whole thing off. Me and the boys just had ourselves a skinful," he said. The moist gum made sucking noises as he spoke.

"I asked Joe to get rid of the Assessor so's I could come in personally and apologise. If he's not giving you enough money..."

"Don't worry, he's been very good," said Mary. "I think you could say it's been sorted out."

"Well, what I wanted to say was: me and the boys would have

made up the rest," said the Moose.

Remembering his manners, he took the gum in his fingers and patted it into the dustpan at his feet. The radio saved them from an embarrassing silence.

"I'm just having a cup of tea, if you'd like one," said Mary, and then, remembering that Moose was Canadian, adding "I'm afraid we have no coffee."

"Tea will be fine, ma'am."

Mary disappeared into the kitchen, and Moose listened to the deepening rush of the filling kettle, and the clank as it was placed on the gas cooker. She emerged, drying her hands with a chequered towel.

"So. Your man Joe Gandelli managed to break it up last night. My knight in shining armour," said Mary, casually. "The pair of you seemed to know each other."

"Me and Joe go way back, ma'am. We were together in Honolulu and Pearl Harbor, although not on the same ship. Joe's was one of the first that got hit. They thought they'd got all the survivors off when they heard hammering behind a jammed bulkhead. Joe went right back across the ship. There was fire, and they took a second hit astern, but he wouldn't let up until he sledgehammered that door open. Saved 15 guys that day. Made him a goddamn national hero," said Moose.

"I'm sorry ma'am," he spluttered, excusing his colourful turn of phrase.

"They transferred us out of the Pacific after that. Now Joe's a bona fide legend with the whole navy. The whole Shore Patrol couldn't have broke up that fight last night – but one word from Joe Gandelli was enough."

Mary fetched the tea from the scullery. As she handed Moose the cup, she could see Gandelli and the sailor chatting with a group of servicemen in the street.

"It was just that I've never seen him before," said Mary, trying hard to make it sound like smalltalk.

"Well, Joe keeps himself to himself, ma'am. He's Italian Catholic, don't care too much for public bars and liquor. He's not out looking for girls, not like the rest of the crew. Sometimes we tell him he'd have saved those 15 men, but let the women drown."

Mary raised an eyebrow.

"Oh Joe ain't *abnormal* or nuthin'. He just don't *apply* himself like we do." The Moose smiled.

Mary noticed the sailor's rifle, still standing behind the bar. He had been distracted by his efforts with the refuse sack, but leaving a weapon unattended was still a disciplinary offence. She lifted the rifle to place it out of sight behind the kitchen curtain.

The Moose rose to a half-standing position, and reached across the bar. "Hey little lady – just be careful with that thing. For all we know, might even be loaded today."

At the words 'little lady', Mary stopped in her tracks.

Pointing the muzzle of the gun to the roof, she deftly unlocked and stripped back the magazine cover, checked the ammunition, and snapped it closed again, in a single motion.

"Loaded all right," she said, and handed the gun to Moose. Picking up the flowered china pot, she walked down the step to get more tea.

When Joe Gandelli came back through the door, Moose was chewing furiously on a new stick of gum. He still had the rifle, clenched tightly in his hand.

"Hell Moose, you look like you just seen a ghost."

"Maybe I have, Joe. Mmmm ... Miss Black just stripped out this rifle and checked the ammo like a veteran. Never saw a woman handle a gun like it before. Now where the hell do you suppose she learned to do that?"

Joe Gandelli put his arm round the Moose, and turned him towards the door.

"Moose, in Derry, there are some questions that you just don't ask."

2

LONDONDERRY, THE FOLLOWING DAY

When the phone rang in Mulhern's Bar the next evening, Mary thanked Joe Gandelli and confirmed she had received the Assessor's cheque that, by now, was safe in the back of the till.

When he asked her if she'd show him around the city on her day off, she struggled to sound composed as she accepted. "Ok, but none of that awful chewing-gum," she said, immediately chiding herself for sounding gauche. When she put down the phone, she was in greater disarray than after the brawl two nights before.

Thursday was her free day. Joe picked her up at 11 in a jeep driven by a fresh-faced sailor who looked like he had been peeled off some billboard ad for hair tonic. "Herm's headed for the Springtown Camp, we've gotta lift," Joe explained to Mary, as she clambered into the back.

"Storemaster friend of mine down there's got a couple of bicycles for us. We can get ourselves some fresh air. If you like," he said.

Gandelli was looking like a country boy in a red check cotton shirt and denim jeans. A plain blue sweater was looped casually around his waist. The jeep curved into the Strand Road and sped along the one-and-a-half mile route to the navy encampment on the city's western edge.

A warming sun was high in the sky as they caught sight of the rows of iron quonsett huts that served as navy quarters. With their broad, semicircular frontages, the huts looked like metal igloos stretching to the horizon, held together by rusty bolts.

Twenty minutes later, the two of them were pedalling along the back road that ran four miles from the Springtown Camp to the hill of Grianán, overlooking the sweeping beauty of Inch Island and Lough Swilly beyond.

Joe struggled with a disconcerting wobble in his front wheel, which threatened several times to pitch him off the road.

"I hope the fellow who made that bicycle didn't make your battleship as well," Mary called. The road, not much more than a track, was deserted, and there was no danger.

"I can tell you, the ship goes mostly where you want it to," Joe called. "Hey, maybe this bike was made during the last war!"

At the base of the hill leading up to Grianán, they dismounted and walked, pausing to collect wild raspberries from the bushes that crowded the roadside. They reached the ancient celtic fort that stood like a flat, round pill-box at the summit. Joe spread his sweater for Mary to sit. They settled to take in the view.

"You know, I shouldn't really be up here. Over the border, I mean. The Irish Republic being neutral and all," he said.

Mary laughed. "I could have you thrown in the brig! Wouldn't that be a scandal. Fine thing to happen to a war hero!" Joe looked at the island below. He did not reply. Mary noticed with pleasure how talk of his famous past made him uncomfortable.

"Actually, down here they turn a blind eye, as long as you're not in uniform."

"So what about life in Mulhern's Bar? Are you going to tend bar forever?" he said, changing the subject.

"Well, I'm only twenty-two. Someday, once this war is over, I want to go away. Take a steamer to Italy or France. Dip my feet in the Mediterranean Sea."

"And pull beers where it doesn't rain so much!" said Joe.

"Yes. We have an old saying in Ireland. You can always tell when it's summertime, because the rain gets warmer." They both laughed.

"My grandparents came to the US from the Mediterranean," Joe said.

"They were from Sardinia. Me, I've never seen it. I want to go some day."

A thought darted into Mary's mind that left her feeling like an ungainly schoolgirl: "*I'll go with you, Joe Gandelli. I'll go with you to the Mediterranean Sea.*"

She had known this man for barely a day. She shook herself, and drove the conversation back to solid ground.

"You know, from here you can see three counties. Down there, that's Inch Island, which is Donegal. That's Derry over there of course, and back there on the horizon, that's County Tyrone," she said.

"You got a lot of fine scenery here. And it's good to be in Donegal. It sure helps me forget the war."

He reached out and placed his hand on her shoulder. Mary allowed him to ruffle her hair. She closed her eyes, and in the red light she fancied she could see the evening sun, sinking into the ocean in Sardinia.

Joe's voice floated through, from some other place. "Hey Mary Black – have you seen *'Mrs. Miniver'*? It's tonight's show at the base. If you're not too tired."

She made a sun visor with her hand, and squinted over at him. "Walter Pigeon and Greer Garson! I hear it's a good one. Worth venturing into the lion's den to see it." They smiled, both happy that their day together was not over.

Mary did not care that Joe could see her delight.

*****

At the film show, Mary lost herself in the magic of the drama. But with its tale of loss and sorrow in the war, *Mrs. Miniver* seemed far from what she hoped for now with Joe.

She thought of Mulhern's Bar, just across the river. It seemed so far away tonight.

The screen darkened, and the crowd shuffled to its feet to sing *The Star-Spangled Banner*.

The world of Mary Black had been changed utterly. She was surprised at the possibilities now dancing in her head. Perhaps she was foolish, racing forward far too quickly. But to think so many possibilities could exist in the drabness of the city, alongside her own humdrum life.

It thrilled her, and Joe Gandelli was different from the rest. Not just for being American, with the easy-sounding accent of a picture-house idol. He valued her for herself, beyond any notion of what the local women called 'improprieties'.

Joe Gandelli reversed the stereotype, and surprised her at every turn.

*****

The next afternoon, Joe had sponsored four local children for the 'American show', a matinee courtesy of the US Navy. The six cinemas in the city were block-booked for the occasion.

He had promised to call to Mulhern's after five, once the final curtain had been drawn, and introduce his guests.

At five fifteen precisely, Joe ushered two boys and two girls, all in their Sunday best, in rowdy procession through the door.

Each held a white bag clutched to their chest, like refugees fleeing from the city. One of the girls was crunching busily on a fistful of pink and white popcorn. The other three had bags of boiled sweets.

The excitement of the visit to a 'picture house' quickly bubbled back to the surface.

Joe steered the four to the big table and, grinning at Mary, called in mock navyspeak: 'Lemonades. Four. Drinking, for the use of!'

The two boys bustled in behind the table, vying with the girls for the long cushioned seat under the window. An eager barter began, the youngest girl hawking her popcorn for boiled fruits, brandy balls, and small red slabs of chewing gum.

Their heads were brim-full of the afternoon's adventures, an epic tale of war that had played out on the field of battle.

'Hi Joe, can you fly a Spitfire?'

'Hi Joe, can you drive a tank?'

'Hi Joe, do you know Spider Kelly?'

The smallest girl had noticed a certain look that had flashed from Joe to Mary. She had stopped chewing and was observing them intently, building the courage to make some giggling comment.

'Hi Joe, do you love *her*?' she exclaimed.

A clatter of laughter burst from four small mouths at once. Mary tried hard to remain composed, but she could feel the heat rising into her cheeks. She hoped she would not blush.

Joe grinned and busied himself fishing a half crown from his pocket. Mary placed two lemonades on the tray. The jury of four at the window were still sniggering. She was glad to be able to turn away, to pour the second couple of minerals.

As the drinks arrived, the children went back to poking each other, and standing up on the seats to look out the window. Their question was left hanging in the air.

They did not see Joe lean forward to the beer-taps and whisper to Mary: 'Maybe I do'.

*****

The next day was Joe's last day in Derry for a while. He would sail on the 'Londonderry Ferry', returning to the city in four weeks.

Mary had decided it was time to introduce him at home. The pair were invited for tea with Mary's mother at 4pm in her house on Laburnum Terrace.

Joe met Mary at the corner of the Guildhall, and linked on to his arm. The day was fine and, rather than take the bus, they walked together the mile or so up the hill, passing beneath the tall spire of the cathedral.

Joe was eager to make plans for his return. They would borrow a car, and go to Belfast shopping. Mary suggested taking the north coast road and stopping at the Giant's Causeway. She was babbling, filled with the excitement of hearing him speak of times a month in the future. She blocked out thoughts of the danger he faced on the destroyer in the meantime.

Laburnum was a solemn line of three-storey terrace houses. Five or six scampering urchins played happily on an uneven footpath. Mary felt the eyes of curious neighbours, hidden behind grimy lace curtains, as she unlatched the door and stepped quietly into the hall.

Joe stared at the swirling embroideries of patterned wallpaper as Mary slipped off her coat, and threaded it over a hook on the wall. She led the way through the dark vestibule and into the warm parlour. Somewhere in the background, a rosewood grandfather clock ticked thoughtfully in the semi-darkness.

The two women were waiting for them.

"Come in son, you're very welcome," said Rose Black. "And this is a neighbour of mine, Mrs. Lynch."

"Mrs. Lynch, nonsense. You call me Peggy. And it's a pleasure to meet you. Mary has told us so much about you," said Peggy Lynch.

Mary raised an eyebrow. She had told Peggy Lynch precisely nothing at all. But it was no surprise that someone had.

She stepped into the kitchen to fetch the tea.

Joe lowered himself on to the sofa, and looked around the living room. The bright orange embers of a coal fire filled the grate.

In the centre of the mantelpiece, four swirling ballerinas twirled inside a bell-jar clock, behind which several ragged brown envelopes were stacked against the wall. Beside them, a wicker St. Brigid's Cross, that looked like it had been made by a child, pointed towards a spiral mahogany candlestick with a lacklustre pewter crown. A background scent of camphor betrayed the use of mothballs somewhere in the house.

"Thank you for inviting me to your home, Ma'am," said Joe, easily. "It's a nice change from the rec room on board ship. It's a treat for us to see real people for a change, after a month at sea."

Rose nodded. "And you so far from home. Which part of America are you from?"

"I grew up in New York, although my grandparents came from Sardinia, originally. Guess I'm a bit of a half-breed, like most Italian-Americans. We had plenty of Irish in our neighbourhood also. Although I didn't know anyone name of Black," said Joe.

Mary entered with a tray and sat it on a pouffe in front of the fire. Joe could see his reflection in the ornate silver teapot which had been borrowed from Peggy for the occasion. Beside it, on a matching silver salver with a paper doyley, sat five plump slices of rich fruit cake. On a white china plate lay a slab of butter with the imprint of a flower on the top.

A formal silence descended, and the monotonous tack-tack of the grandfather clock swelled to fill the room.

Mary poured four cups of ruby tea. 'Strong enough to stand your spoon in," she said, more to chase away the silence than to make conversation.

"Mam said she'll read our teacups when we've finished. It's like telling your fortune," said Mary.

Joe nodded politely, with a blank look of incomprehension.

Rose proffered the cake. Joe had no taste for sweet things, but took a slice, rightly suspecting it had been specially baked for the occasion.

Mary milked their tea. Joe ate his cake, his hand cupped under his chin to catch the crumbs.

"Is it New York you're off to tomorrow, Joe, or will you be visiting us again?" said Rose. Mary winced at the question, as she always did when her mother's curiosity triumphed over delicacy.

"No ma'am, I won't be seeing home this time. We'll make one round-trip Atlantic crossing, docking back here in Derry in one month's time.

"Hopefully to see Mary again," he added, hastily, sensing the reason for Rose's question.

Peggy had finished her tea, and the leaves mottled the inside of the cup, ready to be read. She placed her cup on the saucer. "Right

Rose, I hope I'm going to meet a rich man," she said, peering over her glasses.

"And I hope he'll get here quicker than the last one you saw. I'm waiting for him yet."

Rose took the cup, and tilted it towards the lamp. She frowned thoughtfully, turning the cup in her fingers. "I can see a parcel, Peggy. There's definitely something coming to you. It has money, maybe a bit of jewellery. Are you expecting a parcel?"

"Not this side of Christmas, Rose. Are you sure there's no tall, dark stranger carrying this parcel?" laughed Peggy.

"You're out of luck today," said Rose.

"Maybe Joe will do better," she said, as she reached over to take his cup.

She leaned back towards the circle of lamplight. The tip of her tongue curled between her teeth as she peered into the cup. The white china showed up the yellow nicotine stains on her fingers. "Well, you're going on a long voyage, all right."

"Sure he knows that, Rose," chirped Peggy, waving her hand dismissively. "What about young love's dream? That's what these two want to know," she added mischievously, and Mary winced again.

Rose paused and considered.

"I see a gift for you, Joe. Something given in return. Maybe a reward, something like that. Except that it's ... it's a very unusual reward. Something exquisite and rare," said Rose, meaningfully.

"If it's not an engagement ring, we're not interested," squawked Peggy. Mary blushed profusely, and struggled to swallow her cake.

"No, no, it's not a ring. It's a kind of payment. I can't tell any more than that."

She handed Joe back his cup. He gazed inside, trying in vain to define a single meaningful shape in the damp leaves.

"Right love," said Peggy, reaching for Mary's cup. "Let's see if this is the man for you."

"You stop embarrassing our Mary, Peggy Lynch," said Rose. *You're both of you doing just that*, Mary thought.

"Now, love. Yours had a leave floating when you poured it, and that always means a letter. Good or bad, you can never tell, but a letter will be on the way. Now. You haven't many leaves here. Let's have a look."

Joe took out his packet of Chesterfields and offered them around.

Only Peggy accepted. The ticking of the clock welled up in the silence once again.

"I can see the letter too in the leaves. And there's a figure, a man's figure. It could be either good or bad, but when you get this letter, there could be a journey coming out of it."

Mary prayed Peggy would not mention New York. But Peggy was busy in the embers of the fire, lighting a sliver of newspaper and holding it to the end of her cigarette. The moment passed.

"Well, mam, Joe and I were going to take a walk back down the town. I'm on at Mulhern's at six," said Mary, rising to her feet.

Joe rose with her. "Nice to meet you, ladies. Rose, I hope you'll read my tea leaves again, when I get back," he said.

Mary had her coat on her shoulders, and was pulling on a woollen cap to fend off the cool of the evening. "See you around twelve, Mam."

"See you later, love. And it was very nice to meet you, Joe," said Rose.

Mary and Joe disappeared into the murky hall, and the door clicked closed. Rose and Peggy were left alone in the parlour.

"What a lovely man," said Rose, "and isn't it great to see our Mary so happy."

Peggy could hear a tremble in Rose's voice. It betrayed an unspoken thought.

"Ah now, Rose, I'm sure she's not going to be leaving you for America," said Peggy.

"Too good to her mammy, that girl."

Rose looked away, into the fire. "I always trust the leaves, Peggy. His journey had no end."

"Ah, Rose. They're only the tea-leaves. Not to be taken seriously," said Peggy.

"He seems such a nice man."

*****

Two weeks later a young uniformed courier brought a manila envelope marked 'US Forces Telegram' to Mulhern's, for the attention of Mary Black.

She ripped open the seal and nervously unfolded the soft grey paper. The muddy typing read:

18

See you 20th – STOP – Tall Dark Stranger

Mary's legs were weak and she propped herself against the nearest table. The fears that had filled her head were, with hindsight, silly. Of course they wouldn't have been informing her, if something had happened to Joe. She wasn't next of kin, after all.

Today was the 8th. He would be back in less than a fortnight. She would buy a new dress. She would get her hair done. She would be waiting for him on the quay. She would look like Barbara Stanwyck, or Betty Hutton. They were going on the train to Belfast.

*****

LONDONDERRY PORT AT LISAHALLY, JUNE 20TH

When the Destroyer Escort USS Dallas sailed into Lisahally on the afternoon of June 20th, the familiar brown serge coat and red scarf of Mary Black pushed forward through the small crowd on the quayside. She was waving with a bright smile of welcome.

Joe Gandelli hopped from the gangway, almost dropping his canvas kitbag on to the coal-smeared concrete. Laughing, he turned the mis-step into a feigned stagger, as if finding his land legs again.

"Hey! Am I looking at Mary Black or Debbie Reynolds?" said Joe, pointing to her freshly-coiffeured hair.

"Debbie Reynolds nothing! It's Barbara Stanwyck and you should know your movie stars, Joe Gandelli!" said Mary, with mock indignation. "Come on, no rusty old camp bus for you – I have a taxi waiting."

Telesco had followed Joe down the gangplank, and was happily looking on. "Del, you wanna lift back?" said Joe, turning to Mary to see if she minded sharing the car. The three of them bundled into the back.

Joe talked excitedly of the voyage, which had, thankfully, proved free of incident. He seemed full of excitement to be back, and squeezed her to him as they drove. "Hey, now I know what your mother meant – a rare and exquisite reward. Here she is – in the flesh!" he laughed.

From his hip pocket Joe produced a folded pamphlet. "Let's see what's going on in town this week," he said, tapping the front page with his thumbs to level it out. Mary clasped her fingers on his shoulder, and propped her chin on her hands, peering at the new issue of the navy newsletter.

Joe ran his eyes over the first few lines, but Mary had raced ahead of him. Excitedly, she pointed to the bottom of the page. Joe followed her finger and read:

"Have you heard of Miss Steiner? She will draw a character sketch of you in five minutes, on Sunday Afternoon between 4 and 7pm. A famous artist in her own right who has volunteered her services free of charge to our American boys. Have your portrait drawn for the folks back home!!!"

It was Sunday, and it was quarter past five. "Joe, she's there right now! Joe, get a portrait done for me!" Mary exclaimed.

"Hey, I seen the one she did for Marosky last time she was here. She's some scribbler," said Telesco. "Those pictures sure are a big hit with the guys, though – you'd better get over there quick!"

Joe rolled his eyes at the thought of posing for the artist. But Mary would get a kick out of it.

The car swept up to the entrance to the base, parallel to the red and white security boom, and crunched to a halt on the gravel. "I'll freshen up and change, and see you in Mulhern's around eight – deal?" said Joe.

"Hurry!" said Mary, planting two kisses on his cheek as he moved backwards out of the car.

Gandelli and Telesco ambled past the surly guard and into the base. Mary waved through the rear of the taxi as it turned to drive back across town.

By 7pm, Mulhern's was full to the doors. Telesco and the Moose were denied their favourite seats next to the beertaps. Instead, they took up position at the end of the bar.

Mary introduced her friend Lizzie Deeney, and soon the three were engaged in animated conversation. Telesco, a bundle under one arm, was gesturing excitedly at Lizzie, while the Moose chewed on a cigar that would have done justice to Winston Churchill. All three were holding tumblers of bourbon, when Joe Gandelli squeezed his way into the bar.

"Hey Joe, kinda tight here tonight. I hear three DEs come in since yesterday," said the Moose, wrapped in a swirl of blue smoke.

Mary left the pint she was pouring and came to hug Joe. "I have my break in half an hour. Now. What can I get you to drink?"

20

"I'll have what the boys are having," said Joe, gesturing with the white roll of paper he was holding. He unfurled Miss Steiner's caricature. It was unmistakable, even if it was grotesque. Under the caricaturist's hand, his handsome features had been whittled down to an ocean of wavy black hair and a pair of tiny bead-eyes, with a stock-Italian five-o'clock-shadow on his chin.

"Oh, it's so you," Mary called over the general din. "Now don't get it dirty, I'm having that framed!"

Telesco jolted, as if hit by a brainwave. He sat his glass down, and took the soft suede satchel from under his arm. "This calls for a shot!" he said, unbuttoning the bag and producing a Kodak Box Brownie. "Let's get it now while the light is still good!" he called, parking the half-smoked Chesterfield in an ashtray.

Joe, Mary, Lizzie and the Moose lined up in the small gateway that led behind the bar. Joe held the drawing at his chest, and turned his head for a side-profile. Lizzie pulled up the side of her skirt and tilted back her head, like a flamenco dancer.

Three GIs, who had spotted the camera, pushed raucously into the shot, dropping to their knees in front of Joe, arms spread wide, like a trio of vaudeville singers. "Everybody say Jane Russell!!!" cried Telesco, unleashing a chorus of gleeful whoops as he took the snap.

"Hey Mary," said Joe, rolling up the scroll and threading a rubber band around it. "I got a 'pass out' for tonight – in case we want to celebrate later on. Maybe we can have ourselves a little drink here after the doors close."

"Even better, we're invited for drinks at Lizzie's flat. I already told mam I'd be late. Moose said he has a pass out too. Looks like he's more than welcome to come along," she laughed, nodding at Lizzie, draped around Telesco and the Moose, with the cigar in her mouth. She was coughing and spluttering helplessly. Telesco, his cap at an impossible angle on his head, jostled for room to immortalise the moment on film.

Two hours and a lot of bourbon later, Telesco, who had no 'pass out', lurched towards the door, arm in arm with several other sailors, to be back at base at curfew.

By half past eleven, Mary had cleared and cleaned the bar and stepped into the cool night air towards the taxi outside. Joe was helping the Moose negotiate the double step from bar to kerb. Lizzie, now with the Moose's cap on her head, stumbled along behind.

In the taxi, Lizzie slid on to the Moose's knee and serenaded him tunelessly:

"Wrong, would it be wrong to kiss,

Seeing I feel like this

Would it be wrong to try?

Wrong, would it be wrong to stay

Here in your arms this way..."

She trailed off in half-sentence, and nuzzled into his neck, where she remained until they had arrived at her tiny flat on Park Avenue. Not many single girls could afford a flat of their own, but Lizzie had a good job as supervisor in the telephone exchange.

In the flat, Moose produced a bottle of Wild Turkey, which looked as if half had already been liberated at Mulhern's. He and Lizzie set about demolishing the other half, and within an hour were asleep in an undignified pile on the faded red sofa. Lizzie's gentle snores emerged from where her head was lodged, under the Moose's arm.

Mary and Joe were necking on the armchair by the hearth, although no coals burned in the empty grate. Mary kissed Joe on the lips, then stood up. She took him by the hand, led him into the small bedroom beyond, and closed the door.

*****

The following night, Telesco came into Mulhern's to pick up the soft camera case he had left behind. He was carrying a large package tied up with string and wrapped in brown paper.

"I have something here for Mary," he said to Seamus, Mary's stand-in barman.

"She's not on until eight," Seamus muttered in reply, scarcely disguising his disapproval of local women consorting with the navy men.

"I'll call back," said Telesco, and strolled off to get a beer in the City Hotel.

When he returned just before nine, Mary was busy wiping down the bar. Another destroyer escort had come in that day. The bar was full, it was looking like an eventful night.

"Any sign of Joe?" Mary asked, frowning. His absence, after the intimacy of the previous night, made her nervous, and her nervousness was written on her furrowed brow.

"Something's come up," said Telesco.

"When he got back to base this morning, there was a telegraph message from London. He's to be awarded the Purple Heart. For valour and bravery on the field of battle!" he exclaimed, saluting extravagantly, and standing to mock attention.

Mary's deadpan face flattened his cheery tone. "It's for Pearl Harbor. All the boys are going crazy about it – it's a real honour, Mary."

"I'm sure," said Mary, looking away.

"Thing is, they're flying him out tonight to New York, he's on his way right now to Coleraine to hook up with a plane from there. It's just for a week or so, but he has to attend a few functions afterwards. Might be ten days or so, before he can rejoin the rest of us on ship. Don't take it so bad, Mary. Uncle Sam needs his heroes right now," said Telesco.

"Just a couple of weeks. He asked me to give you this."

Mary did not open the package until she was at home that night. It was a pale green gabardine coat, with a pencil-written note folded inside.

"Mary –

Del will have told you about the medal. This is great news for me. It means four weeks more of being apart for us. But I promise I'll be back, probably some time in early July. Soon we won't have to be apart any more. Until then:

"I'll be looking at the moon –

But I'll be seeing you..."

Your buddy, Joe."

The tune from the Dinah Shore song floated through her head. This was good news for Joe. She was angry at herself for being disappointed.

She dried her eyes, as she slid under the bedcovers.

"So this was your reward in the tea-leaves," she said to herself.

Her words melted into the dark, as she drifted into sleep.

3

NEW YORK, 1943

Joe Gandelli had left his mother as she passed into a fitful sleep, and stepped into the adjacent ward of the clinic, which was unoccupied.

He sat at the end of the neatly-made hospital bed, and stared out the window at the mid-morning sunshine over the Manhattan skyline.

"Nine months. A year at most," said the sallow-faced cancer consultant who stood before him. Dr. Kurt Salinger had a summer cold and the congestion could be heard in his voice. Behind Salinger a junior medic, there only to witness the discussion, looked down at the ground.

"The cancer is not just in her throat," Salinger continued.

"There are secondary tumours near the heart, and in her spine. To operate would be useless. The chemotherapy will slow it down, but that's all." Experience had taught Salinger that most people wanted to hear it straight. Besides, he'd never had much of a bedside manner to begin with.

Gandelli covered his mouth, as he felt his lips tighten.

"Thank you," he said. His voice was remarkably calm, but he wanted to scream.

They were telling him his mother was going to die, and he was thinking it sounded like a scene from a radio drama.

Salinger sniffed, and said: "We'll give you a few moments alone." The two white coats stepped out through the curtain and shuffled across the empty room into the corridor beyond.

Three minutes later, Joe Gandelli composed himself, picked up his copy of the 'New York Times', and followed them out.

Salinger was nowhere to be seen. The junior medic was leaning on the reception desk, chatting with the nurse. 'I'm going home. It's been a long night,' he said, leaning just a little closer than was necessary.

Gandelli walked past the two of them, towards the lift. The junior medic leaned back on the desk, delaying his departure, not wishing to share a lift with a man who had just had terrible news.

Waiting at the lift door, Gandelli looked back out over the city, at the grim line of buildings standing like broken teeth along the Hudson. The irony of it all. They could build these giant monuments to human endeavour, but could not stop the cells consuming his mother's body.

*****

That night, Gandelli lay staring at the roof of his apartment, unable to sleep. Outside it had rained, and a melancholy silence lay over the dank streets of Queens. He squinted at the clock. It was nearly 6am.

He knew he would not sleep now. He felt sweaty and uncomfortable. Better to get some fresh air. He pulled on a pair of jeans, a sweater and a heavy overcoat, and went downstairs.

Steam was rising from a manhole outside in the street. Gandelli crossed Vernon Boulevard, and headed towards the East River. Reflected neon lights lay like streaks of coloured paint on the rain-soaked tarmac.

An early morning mist was floating over Roosevelt Island, and a cold dew was in the air.

A visit to the past would help him come to terms with what Salinger had said. He tacked to the left, and headed for the waterfront.

Walking to the river, Joe thought of the Moose, for whom nothing seemed to complicate the gradual passing of time. Problems seemed not to disturb his good humour. Today, Joe envied him.

He came to the jetty to find a rough-hewn wooden board at its entrance, the word 'Danger' painted in white. The lettering was mottled and cracked, where flakes had fallen to the ground. The board was fixed at a slight diagonal between two sturdy gateposts, at roughly chest height. Beneath it, a padlock and chain, tinged orange by the damp New York winters, held a rickety gate fast shut.

Joe walked over and with his sleeve, dried the flat top of an iron bollard several yards from the jetty. From here, he could see the waves lapping in to the rust-red girders under the quay.

He felt the ghost of his late father emerging from the clammy mist that was fetching up from Brooklyn Heights. The old man looked tired as he took a seat on the bollard beside his.

"They've locked the gate. Looks like we can't walk along the jetty any more," Gandelli said.

"The jetty is old. Maybe a couple of spars have fallen," his father replied. In his left hand he had the hazel stick he used to scratch and draw on the ground.

"Still, you and I see the jetty like it used to be." He held his head bowed and scraped the damp clay between his feet. He was working up to the important question.

"How is she?"

The question was expected, but Gandelli still felt a shock, as if his father's words were a knife that had cut into him. The old man's quiet voice rang like thunder booming in across the river.

Joe gazed at the pebbles speckling the sand, fifteen feet below. Seeing his father, it was as if the pebbles he had thrown as a boy had washed back up again.

He looked across at the island. "She's not good. The tubes to the pump are shot. Nine months. A year, maybe. She doesn't know."

His father drew a circle, turning it deeper and deeper with the pointed twig. He did not speak. In Joe's words, he could hear anger at the disease, but also fear. With both of them gone, Joe would finally be alone. Nothing above him but the sky.

"I'll be waiting for her. You have to move on. They're calling you a hero now."

Guiseppe Gandelli had never used the word 'son'. Their relationship had been too awkward, too reserved for that.

"I don't know many heroes. How do they feel?" said Joe.

The old man's weathered face crumpled into a smile. "Mostly, I guess they don't feel like heroes at all."

He held the stick out in front of him and stared at its tip, like a water-diviner.

"You remember Gino Santini? When you were young you heard me and your mother speak about him at home. Longshoreman from New Jersey. The closest thing we had to a local 'don'. He helped me and your mother, when we came off the boat in 1905. He was a good man, a good Italian."

"I remember. He came over from Brescia."

"Right. Well, when you were about eleven years old, I lost my job in the cement factory, for trying to organise. To get the men into the union. It left us just about broke. The night I got fired, the boys took me for a few beers, and some hotshot started bad-mouthing Santini in the bar. I was angry before I even got there, so I hit him. Then he hit me harder. Damn near broke my face. You remember that?"

Joe chuckled. "Sure I do. You had a head like a beef tomato for a month."

"Well, get this. Years later, I find out this hotshot had been paid to say what he said. Who paid him? Solly."

Joe looked round. "Uncle Solly set you up?"

"Solly set me up. But think about it. Solly knew I was real pissed about getting fired. He knew I'd probably slug that guy. He also knew that Santini would hear about me defending his name. Either that, or he made *sure* Santini heard, I never knew which. What I do know is: inside a week, I had a job at the longshoreman's union. Right outta the blue. That job damn saved our skin. All because Solly arranged for some *farabutto* to do my face over."

"So how come you're tellin' me this now, papa?"

The old man pointed across the river with his stick. "Because you are looking for heroes in the wrong place. The real heroes work like Solly did. Quietly and in secret. I've been watching. I've seen you take the opportunity that Pearl Harbor has offered you, and I know you want to work it, build on it. For your kids, if you ever have some. That's what's makes you a hero."

The sun was rising behind them by now, the first gulls were gliding in, like paper bags on the damp March wind. A ferry sculled up towards the West Channel, nosing behind the island to the terminal at East 63rd.

"So. What are your plans?"

"I'm going to make one more crossing with my ship, then request a transfer back to New York to be with mom. They want me here anyway. Ike himself told me I'm more valuable here, helping with the propaganda war. Kind of a figurehead."

"And your girl in Ireland?"

"When I found out mom was sick, I sent Mary a telegram to say I might not be back. I didn't say why. I asked her if she'd come to Queens, but my feeling is she won't. She has a mother too."

The deep sound of a ship's horn came floating through the mist.

Joe Gandelli looked out to Roosevelt Island. A flock of seagulls was following a barge full of millet. They dipped and circled like a snowstorm.

Joe didn't look round. He knew his father had vanished again.

*****

Manny Janssen was proud to have a hero of Pearl Harbor in the apartment block he minded in downtown Queens.

Knowing Joe Gandelli was a high point in his sad and lacklustre life.

Some called Manny unpleasant and vindictive. The way he saw it, he was just good at a job where conflict with your customers came with the patch. Joe Gandelli, however, he treated well.

When Gandelli entered the lobby, Manny's bulbous little head would emerge from the portal of his office, a lick of over-oiled hair brushed forward in a way that only accentuated his baldness. There was a cunning sparkle in the small, red-rimmed eyes.

Life had placed Manny at the bottom of the pile, and for fifty-four years, that was where he had remained.

Manny played up his acquaintance with Gandelli every chance he got. The staff of the pickle stall on the corner were convinced the pair were bosom buddies. When Joe moved in, Manny had collared him for a photograph, the two of them holding the certificate for Gandelli's Purple Heart.

Manny had the picture on display under the light bulb in the lobby. He would have kept it in the back office, where he spend most of his time smoking and listening to the radio, but passers-by would not have seen it there.

Like all men who have been left short in life, Manny Janssen had a reservoir of bitterness at his core. It spilled out when he could snipe from cover, when his enemies had no prospect of knowing who did them harm.

So when Joe Gandelli announced he was moving back home to live with his sick mother, Manny took the news as a personal slight. The small red eyes narrowed, the twisted mind turned to petty thoughts of revenge.

A personal letter that arrived for Joe Gandelli two days after he left gave Janssen his chance. The air mail envelope from Derry,

Ireland went through the metal door of his coal burner. Janssen snickered as the blue paper was devoured by the flames.

Janssen did not think of reading the letter first. If he had, he would have been gratified by the damage he had done.

As it was, no-one would know that Mary Black had asked to come to New York, because she was carrying Joe Gandelli's child.

*****

Four months later, Manny Janssen snickered again when he saw a familiar face in the morning paper. An air attack on the USS Detroit off Hawaii had left Gandelli, at the eleventh hour of his naval career, in a sick bay with a shard of Cleveland steel in his leg.

For the nation's most decorated Pearl Harbor hero, the war was over.

*****

Two months after Hawaii, Joe Gandelli greeted with bewilderment the news that he was to be awarded a second Purple Heart. In the letter they said 'for valor above and beyond the call of duty'.

On the phone from Baltimore, the Moose had said: 'Must have been because you didn't struggle on the stretcher'.

The fact was, the more accolades he had before Eisenhower rolled him out on the public relations circuit, the better.

After two and a half months on his back and another month on his backside, he was wheelchaired in to a special presentation at the White House. It was followed on the wireless by avid listeners from Vancouver to Orlando. Ike, gratified to be well ahead in the war, called him 'son', patted him on the back, and handed him a certificate that was identical to the first.

He had whispered to Joe: "Son, one good thing about us vets is that we're as useful half-dead, as when we're in the field."

Then, armed with a pair of standard-issue US Navy crutches and a standard-issue US Navy after-dinner speech, Joe was rolled away on a two-month tour of US bases overseas. It did not, he was relieved to find, include Derry.

From Hawaii to Honolulu to London and Berlin, Gandelli carried the President's message to the troops, rubbing shoulders on the way with Bob Hope, Dorothy Lamour, and Barbara Stanwyck.

His encounter with the latter led to press rumours of 'an affair with a celebrated B-movie actress' which, although unconfirmed, did not sit well with his handlers back at the Defence Department. Barbara Stanwyck, for her part, was more annoyed by the 'B' than by the suggestion of the secret liaison.

In his speech, written by the Navy Chief of Staff's office, Gandelli stood on three continents praising 'the indomitable spirit of this great nation of ours', and wondered where that spirit had been when his father got fired from the Brubaker Cement Works, for asking for a decent day's pay.

When he touched down at Idlewild in early 1945, hopes of a final victory were high. His face filled the cover of Life magazine, leading a report that billed the nation's war heroes as 'The Men who Built America'.

Within days, the White House called on him again. This time he would guest at the presidential dinner for the American Banker's Association, an annual event designed to court the men who held the nation's purse strings, and keep the dollars flowing for the Eisenhower administration.

One such custodian was Simeon Haberman, chief executive of the corporate finance division of Swiss Security Bank.

Haberman had made a point of meeting Joe in person. He liked the combination of US military hero and second-generation immigrant from Europe. It suited his bank's image of old-world values: integrity, probity, security, and strength.

And with his affable manner and sports-star good looks, Joe Gandelli would appeal to Haberman's senior executive clients very well.

The following Monday, Haberman received Gandelli at the bank, for what he called 'an informal chat'. With Joe still reeling from the sumptuous splendour of the marble fountains in the reception hall, Haberman offered him a cup of coffee and a vice-presidency.

If he accepted, he would assist the bank with 'marketing', a euphemism for meeting top clients, attending meetings and conferences, and 'pressing the flesh' downtown and on the corporate circuit.

Conscious that, with the war coming to an end, the navy would be letting him go, Gandelli accepted at once.

They gave him an office with an oak desk almost as big as his old apartment in Queens, and hanged his Purple Hearts above it on the wall.

Propped at the window by the desk, almost hidden by the heavy linen curtain, stood an item that Gandelli had brought in himself.

It was an old, twisted hazel stick.

4

New York, early 1945

Hanson Vails was angry.

Angry at himself. Twice in one morning he had indulged in 'conduct unbecoming' to a senior executive of Swiss Security Bank. Personal rancour had taken over, and he had showed his irritation. He knew it, and it riled him.

Vails was a career man and a Harvard MBA, a 'guru' regularly consulted by Wall Street and the newspaper that carries its name.

He had taken 27 years to work, slowly and painstakingly, up the ladder, and he was one of those at Swiss Security who resented Joe Gandelli's fast-track to the top. Haberman had made a good PR move in hiring Gandelli; but whisking him straight to the fifth floor had been a psychological *faux pas*.

Vails was not the only one to resent Gandelli. The golden boy's arrival also rankled with many of the bank's vice-presidents, who could see he had no knowledge of the business. This was window-dressing, pure and simple. Gandelli was there to keep Swiss Security in the society columns, and gain honourable mentions in the gentleman's clubs of Madison Avenue.

But Vails was more angered than most, for his own reasons. Twice he had been passed over for a vice-presidency, and had leveraged his contacts at the 'Journal' to raise his profile at the Bank. Six times in as many months he had been quoted by them as a banking 'maven'. One piece, featuring a line portrait of his face, he had promptly framed and hanged in a prominent place in his office.

Vails was a veteran banker, an elder statesman. But he had let the mask slip today.

Twice he had snubbed Gandelli in a meeting with Ganton Barker Ivory, one of the leading law firms in the city, and his premium account.

He had resented it, when Haberman had 'suggested' he take Gandelli along. It stung Vails to be the less senior banker in the room. Worse again, when Ganton's senior partner David Ivory was clearly impressed by the new VP and war hero from the cover of 'Life' magazine, it had enflamed Vails even more. His own residency at the *Wall Street Journal* seemed insignificant by comparison.

When they had taken their places at the table and Vails had opened the meeting with "Mr. Gandelli, shall we get down to *business*?", the tension had crackled in the air like electricity. David Ivory had allowed himself a wry smile that had gone unnoticed by all but Vails himself.

It was the first time that Gandelli had noticed Vails' chagrin. It made him conscious of his own mortality in the rarified atmosphere of the top floor. Certain odd happenings, since he had joined the Bank, suddenly began to fall into place.

There were the memos Gandelli sent to other VPs requesting briefings on their clients. These requests had sunk without trace.

One appointment, to Incorporated Chemical with VP Marty Connors, had been hastily withdrawn. Connors had given Gandelli the cold shoulder in the executive lounge that Tuesday.

It was a veritable gorefest of corporate paranoia. The 'real' bankers saw that Haberman was deploying Gandelli to schmoose and charm a priveledged bag of clients, chosen from the bluest of the bank's blue chips.

No-one was about to anoint Gandelli with knowledge of their coveted clients. Nor would they guide him into the labyrinth they had built around their top contacts.

Was Haberman grooming Gandelli for a client list of his own? The VPs at Swiss Security were feudal lords. They would not relinquish pieces of their fiefdom to an upstart.

They were battening down the hatches for an attack.

Gandelli was in no doubt. His 'shelf life' was six months at the outside. He could be back on the street by Christmas, clutching his hazel stick and his pair of Purple Hearts.

Unless, that is, he could pull in some serious business for the bank.

It was time to talk to Haberman.

*****

"Das Geld," said Haberman, in the cascading accent of his native Swiss, "ist ein scheues Reh. Money, we say, is timid as a deer, Mr. Gandelli."

He placed his hand on Gandelli's shoulder and led him towards the large tank of brightly-coloured fish that filled the corner of his office.

"Yes, money is so hard to entice into your keeping. Once there, however, it hardly ever flees. Unless you frighten it, of course. If you do not, you can hold it for four hundred years. Please." Haberman waved Gandelli to a seat, uttering the strange 'mmmp' sound that punctuated his speech, as if he were straining to pick something up from the floor.

They settled themselves on the sofas. A yellow envelope was resting on the teak coffee table. It was an internal mail pouch with a long list of names on the front, which had clearly done the rounds of the building many times. Only Haberman's name did not have a wavering line drawn through it. He unthreaded the string, and spilled two coloured folders on to the desk.

Opening the pink folder, he passed a monochrome photograph across. Gandelli tilted it towards the light, and focussed with a look of exaggerated interest. He was eager to impress.

In the foreground, cattle were grazing in a lush meadow. Behind them, a string of x-shaped wooden trestles carried a spiral of barbed wire across the fields and into the distance. On the bottom right of the picture, the words 'Swiss border at Kreuzlingen.'

"So very timid. That is why my country is totally sealed. Tank traps, wire fences, and explosives shafts at all points of entry."

The next photo showed a country road mottled with square grey slabs, like a miniature chessboard. "The shafts can be loaded with explosives at an hour's notice. A small deterrent for an invader, perhaps. But enough to reassure our timid deer. These pictures I show to our customers, to prove how well we are taking care of their money in Switzerland, Mr. Gandelli."

Haberman made his little grunt again. Over the past month, Gandelli had realised the grunts came when Haberman was preparing to make a stern point.

"And so you see how important it is for the client to know us, to trust us, to feel reassured by us. The very sentiments, Mr. Gandelli, that *you* inspire. That is why I hired you. If you can help a client to trust us, then they will *en*trust us with their business. With their ... money."

Habermann was patronising him with schoolboy psychology.

Another sheet came sculling over the table, black lines neatly typed on the Bank's distinctive cream letterhead.

Gandelli picked it up. His lips opened in mild shock. He looked up, but Habermann had turned away, and was gazing out of the window in the direction of the Brooklyn Bridge.

Gandelli looked again at the familiar names. It was the first time he had seen them together, in a single list. They were the fifteen men he had freed from the jammed bulkhead on the destroyer in Pearl Harbor.

Haberman continued, without looking at him, as if addressing some point in the middle distance.

"You will be aware by now that not all welcome you to Swiss Security, Mr. Gandelli. There are those who feel that you have been – shall we say – favoured because of your celebrity."

Haberman gestured towards his aquarium. "They circle like my piranhas. Waiting to catch you off guard. The public's memory is so tragically short, Mr. Gandelli. Your fame can protect you for only so long."

Gandelli looked at the piranhas. He had thought they were some bloated cousins of his late mother's goldfish.

He was relieved that Haberman was aware of the problem with the other vice-presidents.

"Mmmp... these men you saved will be the solution. Right now you need allies. Theirs is the strongest allegiance of all: born from the fear they felt for their lives."

From the purple folder, Haberman produced a sheaf of documents on yellow paper.

"I have had the necessary background checks done to assess which of these men can be of most use to you. Through a – shall we say – *investigator* I use from time to time. He is most thorough."

"With respect, sir," said Gandelli, "I would have appreciated knowing those checks were going on. These men are comrades. They are like brothers to me."

Haberman's tone was dismissive. "Brothers-in-arms, Mr. Gandelli. That is all. I wager you have not seen them since. Mmmp there is absolute no need to worry. My man is very discreet. Like...

a Swiss bank." His shoulders shook with mirth at his own levity. Gandelli's face remained impassive. His clear irritation was a matter of total indifference to Haberman.

"Two of these men will be of value. One is Mr. Hobbs in Cleveland." He thumbed through the yellow sheets, which bunched at the top right, where photos were stapled in a thick wad.

"Mr. Hobbs' father is the chief financial officer with Cleveland Steel. He will help you gain an introduction. The senior Hobbs will be eager to meet the hero who gave him back his son."

Cleveland Steel. Gandelli felt a twitch in his wounded leg at the mention of the name.

"The other is Mr. Veltmann of the building products empire. Both these men you will contact. I take it you are on good terms."

"Yes, Sir, with Hobbs more than with Veltmann, but I know both of them well enough."

"Excellent."

Haberman reached him the two relevant pages. Then he produced another sheet from the pile.

"Which brings us to ... mmmp ... Mr. Rubin. Yes. We also have to speak about him. Mr. Rubin could be ... something of a problem, Mr. Gandelli."

Frank Rubin was a schoolteacher, and had seemed a decent skin. Gandelli wished he could read Haberman's face.

"In the last few weeks, Mr. Rubin has been, as they say in America, 'busted'. During a raid on a private house party in Salinas. He is to be tried on a narcotics charge."

Haberman did not move his head, but looked at Gandelli to gauge his reaction.

"This in itself is not so tragic, Mr. Gandelli. Narcotics and the use of ... I believe it was cocaine ... is more accepted in high society than the authorities would wish. No. That is not the problem. The graver issue is that the party he was attending was of an immoral nature. To be exact, it was ... an orgy. A sex orgy. A *gay* sex orgy."

Haberman peered benevolently over his small, round glasses, like a kind old toymaker.

"He was not a close friend, Mr. Gandelli..."

"Certainly not, sir. I just knew him as one of the men."

"He was *not* a close friend, Mr. Gandelli."

Haberman's pupils had hardened, and the points of his teeth were visible.

This was not a question. It was an order.

"No, sir," said Gandelli, realising that Haberman owned him. "He ... was not a close friend."

*****

Joe Gandelli was smiling broadly, as he stepped out of the lift in the Cleveland Steel building that Wednesday afternoon.

Standing in reception, Roy Hobbs did not notice. He was looking at the female colleague with the armful of file folders, walking at Gandelli's side.

Carmina Cara was a senior manager at Swiss Security, on a level with Hanson Vails, although fifteen years his junior. Her beauty had played only a minor part in her ascent. It was her sharp mind and her instinctive understanding of the requirements of her clients that had singled her out.

She knew her blue-chip clients did not favour Switzerland purely from respect for time-honoured tradition. More than this, she understood that there is one subject more important to an executive than his company's money.

His own.

Haberman had hand-picked her to accompany Gandelli to Cleveland Steel. The gamble had paid off.

Hobbs tripped along behind them like a bell-hop, listening to Gandelli's elated account of the meeting.

"Roy, your father's going to present our proposal to the board. He doesn't think there's a problem," Gandelli said. "This doesn't feel quite as good as being given the Purple Heart, but it's damn close."

"Hell, you and your Purple Hearts," said Hobbs. "You know, I'd have been the hero at Pearl Harbor. I was on the wrong side of that door, that's all."

It had been a good day. Haberman would be pleased.

Hobbs looked at his watch. It was almost six. "Let's celebrate. How about Italian? I know a great trattoria."

In the taxi, Gandelli clued Hobbs in on the detail of the meeting.

"Cleveland got in first on so many defence contracts, they swear your old man knew the war was going to happen. Soon, they're going to split the military work out as a defence subsidiary. When that happens, we get to handle the business. Those accounts are bustin' at the seams, Roy."

"With the figures he was talking, it could put Cleveland in the top 20 customers of the Bank," added Cara.

The Cleveland contract was the second success of the week. Two days earlier, the meeting with Veltmann Building Products had been equally positive. Swiss Security would manage the business of Veltmann BP Europe in Italy, a new company shipping concrete and timber for the rebuilding programme after the War.

For the moment, the company's main account would remain with Chase, but a grateful board of directors would 'see what could be done'. Since the board included Gandelli's comrade Stephen Veltmann, his father, Stephen senior, and the uncle, Conrad Veltmann, the prospects were good.

Vails and the rest, Gandelli reflected, could hardly attack him now.

It was time for a bottle of fine chianti.

*****

Before the trattoria, the taxi took them to their hotel. Hobbs waited in the lobby while Gandelli and Cara checked in, and ran upstairs to freshen up.

Gandelli returned first, having traded the sober suit for jeans and a dark blue sweater. After ten minutes, Cara appeared in a white chiffon dress that was at once simple and stunning.

The thought struck Hobbs and Gandelli, more or less at the same time: *she would look stunning dressed in a flour sack.*

The restaurant was perfect – informal, quiet, and cosy. they sat in a booth that gave them privacy for their celebration. "To Cleveland Steel – and 'Boss' Hobbs!" They touched glasses and savoured the fine red.

The third glass gave Gandelli the brass neck he needed to ask Cara a direct question. "What's the tension between Haberman and Vails?"

Cara pursed her lips in a half-smile that said 'thereby hangs a tale'. She turned the stem of her wine glass as she spoke.

"Haberman is a Swiss, but his family is from old Jewish stock in Germany. He had an uncle and aunt who ran a shoe factory in Neustadt. They disappeared mysteriously in 1939. Looks like they were arrested, and sent by the authorities to Poland. It was the last he heard of them, and he is convinced they must be dead.

"Now Haberman suspects the Germans have been routinely 'exporting' their Jewish population to the east."

Joe looked at Hobbs and raised an eyebrow. This was 1945. It sounded a little far-fetched.

"I know," said Cara, seeing their incredulousness. "Nobody's taking him seriously, but he vets all the bank's new clients and I know he's been using his veto to refuse business from Germany, pending the results of his 'investigations'. His assistant, Lisette, reckons he's working through some secret society in Switzerland."

"So what's this all got to do with Vails?"

"The Vails family's real name is Weiss. Landowners and wealthy farmers in Rhein-Hessen. They made a fortune in wine export. Haberman discovered they've been using slave labour from 'concentration camps' set up by Hitler to contain so-called socially unacceptable elements. That includes Jews, socialists, communists, even homosexuals.

"Looks like Vails is his patsy for German treatment of the Jews in Europe. I even heard that Haberman turned down the US business of Kruppstahl, the German steel company, at the end of the 30s."

"So what does he think about our deal with Veltmann? They're Germans too."

"Yes, but the European Veltmanns are old Jewish money as well," Cara said.

"So Vails is facing a glass ceiling, for as long as Haberman is around," said Gandelli.

Cara raised her glass. "You've got it. And that's why Vails has got your number. He thinks you're Haberman's pot-boy. Listen, don't be deceived by Haberman's 'friendly old man' hooey – he's as deadly as one of those ugly fish of his."

Gandelli raised his glass to hers, and Hobbs followed suit.

"Here's to not getting eaten".

*****

Gandelli's mouth tasted of stale garlic. The chianti had been good, the montepulciano had been superb, and the bardolo had been exquisite. But after sleep, they all smacked of a common *vino da tavola*.

He turned his head. Carmina Cara's tousled hair filled the pillow beside him. They were in her room. Slowly, through the fog in his head, the night was coming into focus.

The drunken sex had been mind-blowing, but Cara had revealed a biting fetish that had left him with red bruising on his shoulders, thighs and genitals.

His cramped biceps made him aware that he could not move his arms. Looking up, he recognised his best tie, binding his wrists to the wrought-iron bedpost.

He cleared his throat, and croaked at Cara to wake her. They had a flight to catch. He had a private meeting with Haberman in five hours.

*****

Four hours and fifty-six minutes later, Gandelli stepped delicately into Haberman's office.

He was finding it hard to walk. The pain of Cara's *crime passionelle* had become excruciating.

Good that it would be a pleasant meeting. Gingerly, he slid on to the couch and shuffled backwards to loosen the tightness of his pants.

Haberman was standing at the window, looking down over the business district.

"Excellent results, Mr. Gandelli. Absolute excellent. Two such prestigious clients. An important advantage for Swiss Security. And for you, of course." His mispronunciation of 'ad-wantage' and the missing ending on 'absolute' were the only flaws that betrayed the Swiss speaker.

"It will be difficult for those ill-disposed to oppose you now."

Haberman turned and rested on the window sill. "Come out, my dear."

From behind the aquarium partition, Carmina Cara stepped over to Haberman's desk.

She had not told Gandelli that she too was coming to the meeting. He was wondering what was going on.

"I must apologise for what must seem a rather sinister approach, Mr. Gandelli, but Miss Cara was part of the procedure to vet you in the field. We shall call it 'due diligence'."

"The Swiss are very thorough," said Gandelli acidly. He wondered if the sex had been part of the test.

Haberman made his little grunt. "Now we can proceed to the next part of my plan."

"Do I hear about that, or will it be a surprise too?" said Gandelli, pointedly.

Haberman was impervious to his sarcasm. "With any luck, the war in Europe will soon be over. In six months, we will require an office in northern Italy, dedicated to our customers in the post-war zone. Your two new clients alone would seem to make that an imperative. But there are others.

"Mr. Gandelli, you speak the language, and now you have gone some way to having the *kudos*. As a public face, you are not so well-known there, but your decorations will speak for themselves. Make sure they are on prominent display."

Gandelli shifted on his seat in irritation. This was not a negotiation. Haberman was a slave trader who chose where to ship his slaves.

"I am gratified to hear that you and Miss Cara got on ... so well. She will be assisting you in Milan. For the moment, let us keep the fact of your liaison within these walls. We have silenced your detractors. We must not furnish them with new ammunition to use against you."

So Carmina Cara was to be part of his reward. A perquisite of the job.

The taste of the wine still lingered, bitter, on Gandelli's tongue.

*****

Gandelli and Cara had regrouped and were sipping coffee at one of the less popular delis two blocks from the Bank. It was off the beaten track, and they would not be seen. She had some explaining to do.

"Look, Haberman vets everyone he hires, especially if they're to come into his 'inner circle'. Some day it'll be your turn, checking out some other new kid on the block. He wanted to know you were a team player."

To prove she was straight, she would offer a juicy titbit of information. "By the way, Vails is spitting blood. Turns out he'd been working on Cleveland Steel for over a year. I heard he had a fit, when he heard you'd reeled them in. That only iced the cake for Haberman, of course."

Gandelli was hung over, and not in the mood for internal politics. He tapped his cigarette pack on the table and drew out a single Chesterfield. "What about last night – the 'extras'. Was that your idea or his?"

"That was ... optional," said Cara, taking his cigarette out of his fingers.

"Couldn't you tell?"

*****

MILAN, SIX MONTHS LATER

Joe Gandelli looked at the two half-finished Bushmills on the beside table. He wondered how something that had seemed so delicious six hours ago could seem so repugnant now.

He shuffled into the bathroom and closed the door, before flicking on the light. The bath towel heaped on the floor carried the logo 'Hotel Intercontinental Milan'.

As he was splashing cold water on his face, the telephone rang. He heard Carmina answer it.

"Who the hell was that at 6am?" said Gandelli, when he emerged. She was still sitting up in bed, the phone receiver at her side. Then he noticed the look on her face: stunned surprise. Alarm.

"That was New York," she said, in an undertone.

"It's Vails. They just found him in his car out at Englewood Cliffs. He shot himself."

*****

An hour later, Gandelli and Cara emerged from their taxi on the Via Dante.

There was no need to hide their relationship now. The only member of staff was Signora Andrina, their personal assistant during preparations for opening in two months' time.

That Cara had accepted Gandelli's marriage proposal some days earlier, Signora Andrina would learn in time. For now, she was in some distress.

"Awful. Awful," she blurted towards them as they reached the top of the stairs.

Gandelli assumed someone had phoned from New York and told her about Vails. He was wrong.

"Mr. Gandelli it is all my fault. But I was simply following instructions," said Signora Andrina, scurrying back across the office, talking over her shoulder as she went.

She made for the large fish tank, identical to Haberman's, which had been installed as a good luck token the previous week. Two fish had come with it: an expensive blue tang and an equally beautiful yellow tang, both shipped specially from the aquarium at Genoa.

Gandelli peered into the tank, adjusting his eyes to the grey morning light in the dark office. He could see no fish.

A yellow object lay on the bottom of the tank. It was the severed head of the yellow tang. A glassy eye stared blankly up at him through the water. Her blue brother was nowhere to be seen.

"The third fish arrived special delivery last evening after you left. A good luck gift from the New York office. I put it in with the other two, before I went home," said Signora Andrina.

A cream-coloured sphere glided from behind the green wall of moss that partitioned the tank. Gandelli recognised one of Haberman's piranhas.

He looked down at the remnants of the beautiful yellow tang.

He thought again of Vails.

5

PORTOFINO HARBOUR, NORTHERN ITALY, MAY 2002

The peach curtains swished soundlessly aside, bathing the room in the Italian spring sunshine.

Maria Gandelli felt the yellow light dance on her face and body, as it washed like milk over the cream walls of her bedchamber.

Over the villa, high on the cliff above Portofino, the sky was china blue, and empty save for the ungainly bodies of gulls sweeping in from the Bay of Tigullio beyond the headland.

She was naked as she stepped out on to her balcony, the distance to the cobbled harbour far below veiling her from prying eyes.

And even if she was observed, she did not care. Time and fortune both had treated her well, and she retained the fresh beauty of her twenties, although she was twice that age. A mane of jet-black hair cascaded over her flawless olive back. The gentle curves of her body had only improved as she reached her fortieth year. Her long legs had the creaminess of the marble, from nearby Botticino, on which she walked.

The flat clang of the basilica bell in Santa Margherita floated around the headland. Its hollow peal, drained of colour by the bay between, announced morning mass at eight o'clock.

Maria was carrying a small telescope she had brought from the bedroom. Through it, she scanned the village stirring into life below, and then the azure waters of the bay.

The tall houses hugging the waterfront were ranged in a concave half-circle, following the sweep of Portofino's tiny harbour. Since she moved into the villa six months before, Maria had thought of them as orange and yellow matchboxes, carefully set in a line by some playful child during the night.

Maria moved the telescope slowly along the jetty. Familiar colours drew her eye to the window of the design shop at the bottom of the port. The poster was for 'Collezione Del Cielo', her own design marque, and the summer collection she had launched a week ago at her showrooms in Milan.

The villagers were pleased that Italy's top female designer had acquired the villa on the clifftop. By showing her poster, they were bidding her welcome.

In Portofino, she would be in distinguished company. Above the town, the treetops huddled round the villa where the Italian prime minister spent his summers. In the narrow alleyways at high season, the paparazzi folded out their canvas stools and waited to snatch on film the celebrated visitors to the 'Pearl of Tigullio'. The tiny harbour's guest book had, over the years, gathered names like Onassis, Burton, Taylor, Berlusconi.

Maria guided her telescope back into the cradle of the harbour and lighted on her 120ft motor yacht, gleaming white at its mooring in the mouth of the bay. A tall figure walked into view above the boat on the jetty path, she followed him as he strolled up the quayside. She knew the man as Giorgio, one of the working fishermen from the village. As she watched, he lay down on the ground, face downwards. A weather-beaten arm darted into the water, emerging quickly with a round, flat object that shimmered blue in the sunlight.

It was a large crab that had ventured a little too close to the water's edge. Picking himself up, Giorgio carried the still-wet crab through the door of the hotel.

Maria held her hand steady, eager to follow the conclusion of the episode. In less than two minutes, Giorgio re-emerged on to the cobblestones, pocketing the banknote he had received for his catch. He crossed the square towards a small tavern at the foot of the hill road, and let himself in for an early-morning brandy.

Such happenings were the perfect antidote to a strenuous week of business dealings in Milan, and Maria smiled as she turned and stepped back into the bedroom.

On the left, a large and ornate tiffany lamp stood on a long, gilt inlaid rosewood table. Beside it stood a rollodex and Maria's notebook computer, its cover closed.

A black case lay open on the four-poster bed in the centre of the room. Maria walked to the case, and slotted back into place the high resolution telescopic sight that she had been using to watch the village. The sun reflected as a small point of silver light on the blue-grey barrel of the high velocity rifle that lay in the case.

She lowered the lid, snapped shut the silver catch, and walked into the bathroom.

*****

Maria Gandelli's manner and grace had been learned at the Internat Fantelli, a leading Swiss ladies' finishing school in the Alpine foothills near Geneva.

Her expensive education had been paid for by the monies from her father's memoir of Pearl Harbor, and his subsequent work as a sought-after speaker on the lecture circuit. As America basked in the glory of its Second World War success, Joe Gandelli was a minor national hero.

At the Internat, they had called her 'Mariechen', 'Little Maria', a name which at the age of 17 had frustrated her. Little Maria, the simple, unsophisticated country girl, her grandparents from Sardinia, clumping awkwardly on to the world stage.

Of all her classmates, Anna Tilssen was the most cruel. 'Simple Maria should be wearing a cowbell. Don't get too close to her, or you'll be smelling of the farmyard."

Today, Maria Gandelli smiled at the memory. It had toughened her for making her own way in the world, and after all, she had done better than most, building a business empire along the way.

Anna Tilssen, Ursula von Wilden-Beck, Birgit von Neumair, Sandrine de Langcort. Where were they now, and what would they say if they could look into the villa bedroom and see her other, her hidden life?

In this secret life, she had learned the value of simplicity. She had learned that, for a plan to work, it *had* to be simple.

It had been simple to poison the leader of Argentina's metal union, before his outdated demands plunged the country into a strike.

It had been simple to tamper with the car engine of a crime journalist on Columbia's leading daily newspaper, who had grown too successful in tracking the activities of the Cartagena Cartel.

It had been simple to put a single bullet in the heart of a Finnish mining engineer, who had threatened to report his company for flaunting oil pipeline regulations in the White Sea.

None of the cases had been resolved. None had been linked to Maria Gandelli, the hired assassin, who, due to her public face as a fashion icon, had ample scope for private journeys at a day's notice.

And no-one had suspected her of her first murder, the only one where personal rancour had played a part. Anna Tilssen had been found, her neck snapped, at the foot of the stairs leading into the school cellar.

It was known that she went there for furtive meetings with the boy she was seeing from the village. Curiously, the boy had sworn he had not arranged to meet her that day. The school authorities had downplayed the affair, frantic to preserve its prestigious reputation. Death by misadventure, they had said.

And with that, the book of evidence had been closed.

Simple.

Maria remembered the words of a Swiss genius: 'Ask simple questions; find simple answers. Then you know: you are listening to God thinking.'

*****

Maria stepped out of the bathroom in a billow of steam. She shook her hair, roughly scrubbing it with the towel as she picked up the black telephone on the wall at the head of the bed.

'Alex, you can bring up my morning coffee now,' she said, and replaced the receiver.

Drawing a golden bathrobe around her, Maria moved to the rosewood table and lifted the lid of the computer. She tilted it slightly to avoid the harsh sun, and bent forward as her eyes adjusted to the light of the screen.

She frowned to see 'Mitteilung: Mazurani' at the top of her e-mail in-tray.

A message from Roberto Mazurani, account manager at her private bank in Geneva, could mean only one of two things. Mazurani could request an appointment for a dreary two-hour discussion of her investments. The meetings were a chore, a necessary evil. Maria was happier meeting her designers and building her business, rather than moving money around to reduce tax on the riches she already had.

Or the message could be a communication from Alberto, the go-between in Palermo and agent for her very specialised contracting service.

She wondered if those for whom she had resolved a problem situation might have her clothing designs hanging in their closets.

The irony would have pleased her.

*****

Maria Gandelli's yellow Lambourghini swept through the gates and down the winding sweep of her driveway into the port below. She had a lunchtime meeting at her office in Milan at 15, Via Sant'Andrea, in the heart of the city's fashion district

From Portofino she wound along the coast road to Santa Margherita, its seafront fringed by lush palms and the blackened fingers of the jagged magnolias that stand guard along the bay.

From Santa Margherita she swept along the Ligurian coast through the grimy clutter of Genoa, with its ramshackle apartment houses studding the threadbare terraces above the dusty port.

From Genoa she tacked north, following the autostrada through the oily tunnels of the hills of Piedmont, past signs marking the 45th parallel, and into the lowlands of Lombardy and the Po Basin.

By noon she was in Milan, parking beneath her office building, five minutes from the imperious spires of the Piazza del Duomo.

For the next two hours, Maria conferred with her design director to put the finishing touches to her upcoming winter collection. Then she sat down with the graphic designer who would create the brochure to market the range around the world. This year's theme of rustic elegance was inspired by the simple workwear of her Sardinian peasant ancestors.

The designer covered her desk with the results of the previous week's photoshoot. Tanned mannequins in fine linen suits posed with old-style hunting rifles atop the white bell-towers and barren rocks of the Isola di San Pietro.

Maria had insisted that the women carry rifles, as well as the men. Only Maria the assassin knew the hidden humour there.

Following the meetings, Maria collected mail from her post box at Milan's central post office, and hurried to her city apartment on the Corso Vittorio Emanuele. She laid her documents on the table, kicked her shoes aside, and poured herself a goblet of Tignarello 1997. Maria loved the wine as much as her father did. She could afford to indulge her taste for it more often.

On the laptop, she located the note from Alberto. She printed it out on orange paper, so that it would be easily found later in her briefcase.

They had not left her much time. The message had arrived late on Thursday. Now she had just 24 hours if she was to fulfil the brief, a contract that would take her to Rome. Alberto had apologised for the short notice, knowing, Maria thought, that she had never turned down a request.

At least she would not have to book a plane. The contract was close to home.

She sent her usual curt reply: 'Proposal acceptable on the usual terms.'. More was not necessary. As expected, a courier pack of more detailed information, sent via Mazurani at the bank, had been left by the maid on the piano. Alberto knew that if Maria rejected the contract, the brief would be destroyed unread.

For her part, Maria knew that $500,000 would be wired to Mazurani the next day, and a further $500,000 on 'completion'. Both amounts would be routed through the 'letterbox company' she maintained in Liechtenstein, ensuring the anonymity of all parties involved.

Settling into the red leather armchair, Maria broke the seal on the plastic courier bag and opened the mustard-coloured legal envelope it contained. She laid eyes, for the first and the second-last time, on her newest quarry.

The mark was Giancarlo Longhinotti, a middle-ranking civil servant in the buildings section of the city administration. The reason his photo was in her hands was a leak he had arranged, to Rome's respectable 'Il Tempo' newspaper, documenting bribes for an office development near the moneyed suburb of Parioli.

Certain parties affected – or disaffected – by the ensuing publicity had demanded the removal of this troublesome cog in the machine.

Maria looked at the photograph in the envelope: a grey-faced, bespectacled bureaucrat descending the steps of an anonymous office building. There was nothing to distinguish him from the thousands of others who crammed the Rome Metro every night, swaying in unison as they read their paperbacks on the way to their quiet night-lives in the outer suburbs.

Maria knew the type. Longhinotti would have a picture of his wife on his office desk. Any colleague wishing to hack into his computer need only know the name of his eldest daughter. That would be his password key.

.Maria read on in the brief. Longhinotti was a creature of habit. He would spend the weekend as he spent every weekend: motoring the 80km out of Rome to fish at the Lago di Bracciano, west of the Rome to Bologna autostrada, between Marto and Capidimonte.

Maria Gandelli sipped her red wine, and looked out of her window at the knotted silhouette of the Duomo, rising like a skeleton in the rusty Milan sunset. Tonight, Longhinotti was none of her concern. She was 'Simple Maria', obediently delivering a message for her patron.

This time, Giancarlo Longhinotti was not the fisherman. He was the fish.

*****

On Friday evening, Maria lifted her Gucci overnight bag from the wardrobe. Of her 140 business suits hanging on the rails, 27 had been designed by herself.

She had one minor eccentricity. She liked to match her outfit to her mark. Gucci for a bureaucrat; Versace for a millionaire; and, were it ever to happen, her own Gandelli for a politician or a prince.

She slipped out of her apartment just after 2 o'clock. She left the gleaming blue Ferrari and the Lambourghini in their parking bays, favouring the less ostentatious Alfa Romeo for the long night drive to the capital.

*****

Dawn was breaking over the Roman skyline as Maria drove past Fiano, and began the sweep into the city centre.

Her destination – the Lago di Bracciano – could have been

reached directly, but a detour into the city was vital to the security of the project.

Maria Gandelli did not carry a weapon with her in transit. It had saved her before, it would do so again. If she were compromised due to the unpredictable action of some crazy driver on the road, no gun would be found. It was simple. She was Maria Gandelli, the well-known fashion designer, on her way to a photoshoot on the squares of the city.

She kept her weapons in a network of safe deposit boxes in Rome, Milan, Venice, Naples, Ravenna, Ancona and Pescaro. As part of her 'hidden life', they were not left with the exclusive Banca Sella, who handled her private fortune, but with the Banca di Roma.

Each deposit box contained a loaded pistol with silencer. Each was accessible at a moment's notice. She was one of the best-known faces in the personality magazines, and her offer of personal ID was, more often than not, politely declined. She would be ushered directly to the strongroom, with a respectful whisper from her banker.

At 10.04am, she entered southern Rome's largest branch of the bank. Maria eschewed the offices in the centre, feeling less conspicuous away from the city's traffic maelstrom, in the leafy suburbs.

Left alone in the vault, she withdrew the metal casket, and carefully lifted the black velvet bundle on to the table to her left. Glancing at the almost invisible pinhole camera in the strongroom wall, she closed the box, and folded the parcel unopened into her bag. A fresh-faced clerk unbolted the grille, nodding respectfully as she re-entered the banking hall.

Fifteen minutes later, Maria raised her right hand to her forehead in a blessing, as she swept past the Vatican City towards the lush verdure of the Tolfa Hills and the Lago di Bracciano.

Longhinotti's fishing location of preference was along a dirt track near the medieval town of Anguillara, a lesser-known cove where he could have some privacy, even in the peak season.

Maria pulled in on a ridge, where a break in the bushes gave a direct view of the lake below.

She flipped open the cellphone she had bought specially for the project; its number was known only to Alberto, and it would sink to the bottom of the River Po, when the job was done. As she expected, a text was waiting, which said simply 'Our guest has departed'. Longhinotti had left his flat at more or less the usual time.

Now she had only to wait.

With a binoculars she scoured the track and the tree-line for signs of other vehicles. She scanned the forest floor and the waterline, checking for wanderers hiking the lake. So far, so good. For the moment, there was no-one around.

Once, Alberto had commented on her cold blood and lack of nerve. If she were ever to adopt a codename, he had said, it should be the name of a reptile. This morning, she was as calm as the lone raven she could see sitting motionless on a tree branch further along the lake.

She slipped off the soft badminton shoes she wore for driving, and reached behind the driver's seat. Her father's army boots were two sizes too big for her, and she had stuffed the toes with brown paper. If she was lucky, the larger male footprint would fool the investigators, who would assume they were looking for a man in any case.

She sat the field glasses on their felt pouch, and unrolled the cloth covering of the pistol.

"Don't blame the messenger, just because she kills you," she had once said to Alberto. Today, the comment seemed a little crass. Perhaps she was getting older.

The thought was interrupted by the grunting arrival of Longhinotti's metallic blue Nissan Terrano on the track below the ridge. The flamboyant colour was at odds with the personality of the owner. "We all have our way of going mad, Giancarlo," Maria thought to herself, as she checked the gun again.

She had memorised her intelligence from Alberto. A glance through the field glasses confirmed the Roman registration. She also confirmed the scuff and dent on the front side panel, which had been a gift from one of the capital's more erratic road users.

Longhinotti stretched his legs, lurched out, and walked around the jeep. He drew a satchel from the rear portal of the vehicle, and unflapped it without lowering it to the ground.

Maria frowned. This did not look like the fishing gear she was expecting. And she did not like the unexpected.

Her brow relaxed again, as he walked across to a wooden picnic table by the trees. He placed a large metal thermos and an orange plastic food container on the rough oak.

The thermos had green cloth pads, giving it a military style, and Maria noticed that Longhinotti's fishing clothes, while clearly expensive, shared the same camouflage look.

She smiled to think that men like Longhinotti all had their secret world, the fearless 'other self' behind the meek office worker. If he smoked, he would smoke Camel. And his watch, Maria thought with a smile, would be waterproof to fifty metres, although the only water it has seen is when he shaves in the mornings.

Maria focussed, and took a deep breath. She pocketed the pistol, and walked back along the upper track, towards the main road. After fifty yards she stepped over into the undergrowth and made her way through the mulch and fallen branches toward the lake's edge, before turning left on to the lower path. She could see the fresh treads where Longinotti's jeep had passed.

She was walking into the forest, towards him now. She could see him in the distance, his back to her, his elbow lifting as he tipped the thermos of coffee towards the cup.

Beside him, an unfurled napkin held a hunk of the local *rosetta* bread, with several slices of *caciotta* cheese.

Maria was unconcerned as she strolled over the grass. An attractive woman on her morning walk. When he saw her, he would see no threat.

As she came level with him, Longhinotti nodded diffidently, barely looking up. He gave a barely audible 'bongiorno', and busied himself with his food.

She took her hand from her pocket and straightened her back.

"A tavola non si invecchia," said Maria, as she squeezed the trigger two metres from Longhinotti's forehead.

The old Italian proverb was the last sentence he ever heard.

'At the table, nobody grows old.'

6

Tibesti, Chad, 1975

De Vries could taste dried blood on his tongue. It had poured on to his cheek as he lay on the bunk. It was not his own bunk, and he was not lying in the barrack room.

Without moving, he spat into the small pool of blood he could feel under his cheek. He felt a hard fragment between his lips. One of his teeth had come out.

He did not try to sit upright. His ribs, where they had kicked him, were an agony of fire. His eyes were swollen and would not open. His body felt like it had been hammered flat.

At the previous night's appel, the inspecting officer Sergeant Archat had said the soles of de Vries' boots were not properly polished. He had thrown them disdainfully into a corner.

Any other legionnaire would have been on the receiving end of a hard slap in the face from Archat. This was his normal rebuke when a shirt showed a dirty collar, or the white glove he ran over a bedframe showed dust. A slap in the face, and that would have been the end of it.

Not for de Vries. Archat had it in for him. And he was not the only one. All the legionnaires knew that the real punishment could be left to Walser, Adamsen and Schanz.

Schanz, the big Austrian, was top of the pecking order. A thick-necked bull, the lowest form of human junk, with a collection of pictures in a tobacco tin under his mattress that 'would not interest a normal man'. For him, the French Foreign Legion had been the only alternative to a prison term, for a series of sex assaults in Hamburg and Amsterdam.

Adamsen the Dane had served with the Legion since Philippeville, 1961. After the brutal rape of an Arab girl, he spent six months at the Legion's prison at Colomb-Béchar. It was seen, not as a punishment for attacking an Arab, but for breaching Legion discipline. In a jar of pickle vinegar in his locker, he had the ears of 8 Arabs he had killed in close combat.

Walser was a weak personality who stayed close to Schanz and always carried a *coupe-coupe* machete. They had come to the Legion together. Some suspected they were a couple as they drank at the *bordels*, but never went upstairs.

Most of the company, they hated for sport. De Vries, however, they hated because he came from money.

His family were old wealth out of Lyons with hotels in the dependencies in the Indian Ocean, Mauritius and Réunion. The hotels had always done a fair trade, but the real boom had come when his grandfather built on casinos in the 1900s, catering to the wealthy ex-patriate French who retired offshore.

But now, de Vries' wealth was a millstone round his neck. He had taken three beatings from Schanz and the other two in as many months. He knew he could not take many more.

*****

De Vries felt a wet sponge press against his forehead. Tom Black dried the blood from his lips and told him not to open his eyes.

"Where am I?" said de Vries.

"In the infirmary. Just as filthy as every other place in this hell-hole, but at least it'll get you away from Schanz and Adamsen. For a few days." Black poured some iodine into the cloth for de Vries to chew on. It felt like medical care, but they both knew it would be useless against infection from the flies.

Black was an *ancien* of the Legion, a veteran of 15 years since he had left Derry to join the Legion, at the age of eighteen, in 1960.

Now he had made captain, and he was tired. Soon he would leave the Legion, try his luck back out on the street. The ability to march 20 miles with a pack full of stones, or live for a month on roots and rats, would be of little use there. That was tomorrow's problem.

For now, he had to keep de Vries alive through the last 8 weeks of his own five-year stint.

"Why are you a legionnaire? I heard you come from money," said Black.

De Vries removed the antiseptic cloth, squeezing it lightly between his fingers. "My father and grandfather were both legionnaires. It's a rite of passage for us. Our ticket to the family business. No service – no money. C'est ca – it's that simple."

De Vries groaned as he tried to raise himself into a crawling position. Black looped his arm under his chest to help him up.

"Archat wanted you out on 'tombeau'. I had to over-rule him," said Black.

Five nights on 'tombeau', sleeping in a coffin-shaped hole in the ground, would have drained de Vries to a husk. After that, the first 20-mile march would have achieved what the beating had not. If pneumonia didn't get him first.

"I've never heard of *tombeau* for a minor offence at appel. What has Archat got against you? Tomorrow they're attacking a Libyan camp out near the caves. He was busting a gut to get you along."

De Vries frowned. "Probably needs all the men he can get. I heard there were nine desertions in the last month."

Black tried hard not to smile. How could a man half-beaten to death be so naïve? He was liking de Vries more and more.

"My thinking is you'd have been volunteered to be first into the caves. If there are Libyans in there, you're a silhouette against the sun and they use you for target practice. Not many come out again. Believe me – I've seen it before." He unbuttoned his shirt and pulled it back. Two ugly red weals disfigured his shoulder. "I was in Algeria, at Chélia in 1960. I was lucky."

"Hey, Black. Maybe I will be lucky too," said de Vries with heavy irony. His swollen lips moved slightly into a half-smile.

"You'll need more than luck, for the next month or so. The surgeon here is a good man. I've convinced him to keep you in for a week.

"Now we have to find out why Archat is trying to kill you."

*****

Schanz slipped through the side window of the barrack, and dropped soundlessly to the edge of the parade ground below.

For such a big man, he could move silently as a cat.

He checked his watch. It was 3.13am. The guards on the night watch, which ran from 1 o'clock until 4, would have settled well in to their game of cards. What he had to do would not take long.

Crouching low, he skirted the perimeter at a jog. He was moving counter-clockwise along the north edge of the camp to avoid the arsenal, where extra guards were posted.

The moon was full, the only other movement was the glow of a comet running low near the horizon.

The moonlight worked to his advantage. he could see the occasional sentry above on the parapet; they were not expecting to see him.Their attention would be on the outer wall, watching not for intruders, but for the next deserter.

He paused behind the *foyer*, but the last drinkers had dispersed into the night or the bordel, two hours ago. Now there was silence.

Schanz could see the infirmary a hundred yards ahead, diagonally across the open courtyard to his right. De Vries was the only patient, and the lights were off.

Rather than cut across the parade ground he ran swiftly past Barracks 12 and 13, using their cover to shield him from the direct light of the moon, and avoiding the coffin holes left by this week's *tombeau.*

At the infirmary window, he drew a 2-feet length of cord from his pocket and wrapped it around his right hand. Schanz knew no-one would ask any questions: de Vries, they would say, had been suffering from depression. No-one would be surprised that he had hanged himself from a beam.

He eased himself on to the window ledge. He swung up his legs, turned and entered in one fluid movement.

The first blow crushed his larnyx. With a single, painful groan, he went down on one knee. The second blow smashed the second and third vertebrae at the top of the neck.

Tom Black was already looking out, right and left, from the infirmary window. No guards nearby. Just the moon and the solitary comet spinning onward into the desert.

He did not need to look down. He knew Schanz was dead before he hit the floor.

*****

When Leblanc, the senior surgeon, came in to see his only patient the next day, he did not notice that the reserve crates of iodine and syringes at the back of the infirmary had been rearranged.

Nor did he see the smoothed sand under the wooden decking on which they rested, which betrayed the location of a shallow grave.

Schanz would be recorded as a deserter, and few would mourn his disappearance. Save, of course, a detective or two in the sex crime section of Interpol in the Hague.

*****

"I thought they would hit you here, rather than wait for you to be discharged. You were alone here. It made sense," said Black.

The morning sunshine was filling the infirmary with yellow light. De Vries was able to sit up now. The death of Schanz had given him hope again.

Better still, in the two nights since Black had buried Schanz, news had come in of another desertion. Adamsen really had gone over the wall.

"That leaves that weasel Walser," said Black. "He'll be a frightened man tonight – there are too many old scores to be settled out there. We'll have to get to him quick."

"Walser's sure to desert, if he's got any sense," said de Vries.

"If he deserts," said Black, "that's our last chance of finding out who sent Archat after you."

*****

Adamsen had already been badly beaten when he was thrown out of the military police jeep at the Adjutant's office the following morning.

De Vries was watching from the infirmary window, when Adamsen was brought back in.

He had suffered the standard punishment for deserters.

First, three hours of *la pelote*: running, crawling, marching at knees' bend with a sack of stones on his back, and a metal helmet, the interior removed, on his head.

After this, drained of every ounce of strength and reduced to a babbling wreck, came the final indignity. A forced swim through an open sewer, then a crawl on his belly around the barrack room. An inhuman mess of filth and ordure, totally broken and grunting like a pig, watched by his fellow legionnaires standing to attention at their bunks.

De Vries knew this was nothing to what he would endure later, after his trial, when he was sent to the penal battalions. Endless days breaking rocks under the searing sun, and, sooner or later, *le cafard*: the strange madness they describe as a million beetles crawling around inside your head.

De Vries edged back on to his bunk. For his own sake, he was trying hard not to take pleasure in this barbarism.

But no-one left the Legion with his humanity intact.

*****

"Not a week, de Vries. Three days, four at most," said Doctor Leblanc, closing his medicine bag and moving to wash his hands in the small sink at the wall.

"Don't forget, shamming will get you eight days in 'The Hole'. The ribs will heal. Keep yourself out of trouble for a while."

He hanged his stethoscope around his neck, and smiled. Both men knew that de Vries had not gone looking for trouble. He was five hundred miles from civilisation, and the trouble had come looking for him.

Captain Tom Black was waiting outside, and Leblanc saluted him as he passed him in the door. Black leaned against the wall by the small sink. There was little time for small talk.

"There are four cases of supplies over in admin. I've ordered Walser to bring them here tonight, when they get back from patrol. Around dusk. We'll have to move on him then. Now that he's exposed, he's a big threat to Archat as well. And Archat, as we know, doesn't wait."

"I'll be ready," said de Vries, sitting up on the edge of the bed. His swelling had gone down. He was looking half-human again.

The sun had almost gone as Walser lugged the last crate into the infirmary supply room. He turned on the tap to wash the sweat from his face. It had been a long day, with a pointless 35-mile march along the edge of the desert. They had encountered no-one save the inhabitants of two small farms they had seen on the way.

De Vries approached Walser from behind, and smashed his nose against the wall, crunching the bone.

His fury masked the pain of his healing ribs as he locked his grip around Walser's throat and dragged him across the supply room. Tom Black stepped out of the shadows and between them they lifted Walser off his feet and crashed him down into the chair. In less than a minute he was tied fast, his hands behind his back and his ankles lashed to the chairlegs.

Black tore a length of bandage which he stuffed into Walser's mouth and tied behind his neck. The veins stood up on the German's forehead. The beady eyes bulged in a face apoplectic with fear.

De Vries grabbed Walser's hair and snapped his head back, jerking a half-bottle of iodine into his eyes. Walser bucked and squealed, but the bonds were strong and no-one could hear him over the noise of singing and drinking from the *foyer*, which was in full swing.

"Archat sent Schanz after me. You know why. You will tell me. Now or later," said de Vries, in fluent German. It was the even, cool tone of his voice that chilled Walser to the bone.

Water was seeping from his eyes, and iodine and mucus were streaming from his nostrils. De Vries loosened the gag. The reddish liquid ran into the corners of Walser's mouth. He gasped for air.

"Archat will kill me if I talk to you." said Walser. He was taking his gamble. De Vries was close to going home. He would not risk murdering a fellow legionnaire now.

De Vries did not reply. He forced the gag back into Walser's mouth. Calmly, he produced a small hemp bag from under his bunk and inverted it in front of Walser's eyes. A black object dropped neatly into Walser's lap. It was a giant scorpion.

Walser panicked and reared, bucking so hard that he knocked himself sideways and landed face-down in the sand of the store-room floor. He was gasping uncontrollably behind the gag.

De Vries threw the sack back over the scorpion, and raised it over Walser's neck. The scorpion dropped on to the side of his neck, but slid backwards on to the floor behind his head. The grunts behind the gag grew louder.

De Vries lowered the sack, allowing Walser to calm down, before loosening the gag once more.

Walser was half-babbling, a mixture of shortness of breath and terror. This time, it was not the scorpion that had convinced him. As de Vries leaned to gather the creature up, he glanced to where Walser was looking, behind the stock of crates.

Staring back at them, and raised out of the sand at an obscene angle, was the face of Schanz, one eye and most of the other already eaten by desert ants. A pile of clay showed where someone had tried to dig him up.

De Vries glanced at Black. They would try to figure it out later. Both knew they need say nothing now. Walser's tongue was loose, and he had the floor.

"Archat sold a shipment of Legion guns to the local Frolinat resistance two years ago. He ... he told the Adjutant they'd been hijacked. The Legion would shoot him on the spot if they found out," said Walser, panting.

"Lately he's been seeing an Arab whore, Sehra, who he met in N'Djamena. He brings her in once a week by jeep. A while back they had a bust-up. When he threw her out the gate, she was screaming at him. She called him a fucking traitor, and mentioned the guns," he said.

"What's it got to do with me?" said de Vries.

"He smuggled her out at Tower 4. That was your watch. Archat reckons you must have heard it all."

De Vries let go of Walser and walked over to Black. "That would figure. The night before Schanz had his first go at me, I'd been drinking in the *foyer* all night. I climbed into the tower and slept through my watch. I heard one of the whores screaming something in bad French. It didn't even wake me – I thought it was one of ours from the bordel."

Black's mind was racing. He looked back at the half-devoured face under the crates. "So now Archat knows about Schanz. That could work in our favour. I'll get word to him that you'll deal."

"What about this bastard?," said de Vries. "I could let the scorpion finish him off. Dump him ten miles down the road. It will look like he deserted and was sleeping rough in the scrub."

Black looked down at the pitiful figure on the floor. He had seen a thousand Walsers in his time in the Legion and could read them like a book. Without Schanz for protection, Walser knew he was an easy target. He would present no threat.

"He won't talk, he's too scared. Besides, he has nothing on us, once we've got Schanz out. We have five hours of darkness left. I'll get a jeep, there'll be no questions asked. Then, we can cut him loose and let someone else take care of him. And they will. Poor bastard won't last another day."

7

LA RÉUNION ISLAND, INDIAN OCEAN, 1975

Toto pulled the jeep off the coast road at the sign that read 'St. Benoit', and skidded on to the dirt track that led up the hillside.

On both sides of the road, thick tamarind branches had been snapped like twigs by a fierce cyclone that had ravaged the island two days before, and was now petering out in the Indian Ocean to the west.

Blue water sparkled in the rear view mirror as the vehicle climbed the pass between the island's two volcanoes, Piton des Neiges and Piton de la Fournaise.

Piton des Neiges, Toto told the brown-skinned, haggard man beside him, was dormant now. La Fournaise was not, and towered threateningly at the upland end of the island.

Passing through the lush greenery of Bebour-Belouse Forest, Tom Black found it hard to believe that this island paradise could be transformed into a sea of black ash in a single moment.

The bamboo and plane trees of the forest yielded to a sea of silver-white blossoms along the edge of the De Vries sugar cane plantation. The roadside was dotted with rust-red iron shacks, the homes of the sugar workers who cut the cane and brought it to the refinery at St. Pierre.

Black caught himself scanning the mountainside for caves, watching the tops of the hydrangea bushes for the telltale shuffle of leaves that, back in Africa, might have revealed an Arab sniper. He had to remind himself that the Legion was over. The landscape was benign. It was no longer threatening him.

"How you come to La Réunion, Mr. Black? I hear you an old friend of Mr. de Vries?"

"I think you could say I helped him out with a tricky situation in Africa. The offer of a position here was a debt of gratitude," said Black.

Looking out the window, Black caught the intense colour of a flame tree as they passed. "Toto," he said. Even calling a man by his first name seemed strange.

"It wasn't just Jacques de Vries that wanted me to come. I hear the father practically insisted. Maybe old man de Vries has some plan in mind."

Toto's coal-black face cracked into a broad smile. "Don't underestimate the old man. He's always got something in mind. These days, he has political goals. Maybe he want to become governor, some day."

"Jacques didn't tell me that. Is there much opposition?"

"Only the De Chateauvieux, the other sugar cane family on the island. Two dynasties. We call them the De Cs and the De Vs. Henri de C would have the same ambitions as Monsieur de Vries, but he's rotten to the core. The people are no fools. De C operates with bribes and threats, and he has enemies everywhere. It's a small island."

"And if the father goes into politics, what about Jacques? I guess he's the natural choice to take the hotels?"

"Oh, he's done his time now in the Legion, like his father wanted. He'll own the whole business some day. The hotels, the sugar cane, the coffee, the pineapples, the bourbon vanilla. He goin' to be a rich man. But for the moment, someone from outside is needed. Maybe you are that person. You have no enemies here, only friends. Besides, you an Irish. We all like Ireland." He broke into another white-toothed grin. "Just don't ask us where it is."

They approached the crossroads at the summit of the Grand Bassin plateau, curving across the road occasionally to avoid broken branches from storm-damaged trees. Toto explained that the cyclone had ravaged the plantations, and that the pineapple and papaya harvests would be particularly badly hit.

Suddenly he pressed hard on the brakes, thrusting Black forward to the dash. This time, there was no twisted wood or foliage to be seen. A small, red cloth bag lay in the centre of the road, just at the cross junction.

"Jesus Toto, you're going to kill us."

"Pardon, monsieur, but this bag cannot be disturbed. Not an

offering at the crossroads. Old tradition of the Hindus from the coast of Malabar. They say it wards off evil spirits."

Toto pulled the jeep hard right, making a semicircle.

Black was curious. "What's in the bag?"

"Ooohh, a hundred years ago, it would have been the head of a slaughtered goat, or a dead cockerel," said Toto. "Real bad voodoo."

Again, the white marble of his perfect teeth lit up his craggy face. "Today? Probably a packet of chocolate cookies."

Toto hooted with laughter, slapping his knee with his right hand. "You disappointed, Irish?" he said, as he pulled the wheel to bring them back on to the road.

*****

Cresting the hill, the jeep dipped like a rollercoaster down towards St. Pierre. The town knelt at the foot of the escarpment, just where the land met the deep blue of the Indian Ocean.

From there, they swung left on the coast, driving out via Grand Bois towards Manapany-les-Bains.

Six hundred metres short of the town, Toto pulled in through the gate of 'Savannah', the De Vries estate.

A long, gently curving drive skirted by tall coconut palms led to a gleaming plantation homestead. The fassade and shutters shone with the bluish coral wash that was the trademark of the whole Mascarene Archipelago.

"This land has been the home of the de Vries' for 300 years," said Toto. "Maybe they are the oldest 'gros Blancs' on La Réunion. Grand-père de Vries, *his* grand-père started the sugar cane. Now, they own all the cane you saw today."

Black reckoned up in his head. They had probably passed five thousand acres of cane plant on their way from the airstrip at St. Denis.

"And how big is the de Chateauvieu operation?"

"About a quarter as big as the de Vs. Not getting bigger, like he'd want. As I said, nobody wants to work for him 'less they have to. He still thinks like a slaver. A worker ran off his estate five years ago at harvest time. De C had him bull-whipped. But he has the chief of police in his pocket, so they turn a blind eye."

The door of the mansion opened, and Jacques de Vries stepped on to the verandah. Where Black had expected a welcoming smile, there was only a careworn scowl.

"Tom, good to see you," he said, embracing Black briefly as Toto busied himself with the two large travelling trunks.

"I'm afraid your arrival has been marred by something of a crisis," said de Vries. "We've been fighting fires, quite literally."

"Yes, I saw plenty of evidence of the cyclone on the way from the airport."

"I don't mean the cyclone," said de Vries. "We've had another problem. I instructed Toto not to mention it to you. There's a curfew that comes when cyclone alert on the island goes to level red. No-one on the streets until the storm has passed. Under cover of the curfew, they laid a fire last night at our casino at the Saint Expedit Hotel.

"Toto saw the fire from his house, which faces down to the hotel. But in cyclone red not even the emergency services can come out. It was two hours before we could get help. The casino is destroyed. Luckily, it stands apart from the hotel. Otherwise, someone could have been killed."

"From what I already know, the chief suspect would be Henri de Chateauvieu?" said Black, following him up on to the verandah and into the shade of the house.

"I'm not certain. There were two of them. We rang the police and they brought in two low-lifes from up at *le volcan,* Branco and Cheron."

"A case of 'the usual suspects'?" said Black, settling into an armchair in the large, airy salon.

"Well, we have to start somewhere. We're running a business here, not a charity. We had to lay off 117 fruit pickers a month ago, after the last cyclone hit. Branco and Cheron were among them. There's no shortage of workers with a grudge against us. These two have no connection to the de Cs, though. Unless he hired them to set the fire."

De Vries looked at Black, who was clearly sweating in the heat. "I'm sorry, Tom. Toto will show you to your room. Freshen up, come down, and we'll talk."

An hour later, de Vries and Black were seated in a bright plant conservatory in the back of the house. The sun sparkled through the rich colours of the plants: the pinks of torch ginger, the neon yellow of the allamanda, the dark purple of the bougainvillea.

On a rosewood table stood two white bowls of *cari*, La Réunion's spicy stew, with generous slabs of white bread on a breadboard between them.

Sipping his glass of rum punch and warmed by the heat coming in through the wooden blinds, Black felt remote from cyclones and storms. De Vries' dark mood was the only reminder of the serious matters at hand.

"I thought de C was running for office," said Black, "He'd be crazy to start something like this."

"Oh, he's crazy, all right. It's a streak that's been in the family for a hundred years." The strong punch had calmed de Vries somewhat.

"They say his grandfather loved a half-caste, a singer who made her living singing 'maloya', the old slave blues, in the drinking dens of St. Denis. Say she had a son to him. Well, he had the child killed, and she put a curse on him and the whole de C line. People believe in curses and that kind of thing around here."

"Yes, I saw something at the crossroads. Some kind of voodoo offering," said Black.

"Well, old de C lost his marbles soon after that. It was probably just the rum that did it, but it suited the locals to say it was the curse. He had 60,000 coins shipped in from Europe, with his own face printed on them. Wanted to pay his workers with them, make them the national currency. Some say they're still in two chests at the de C mansion. They call them the 'de Chateauvieu Doubloons'."

"And what about the current de C man?"

"Oh, Henri. Henri is a petty tyrant. He's not liked here, and behaving like a demented feudal lord doesn't win him any friends in Paris either. La Réunion may be a French *departement,* but on the mainland they think we're some kind of banana republic.

"Henri has had his bad luck, too. A few years ago Lisette, his only child, disappeared. This was 1968, just as I was leaving for the Legion. She was 16. There were a few women murdered around the same time. They called them the 'Kali Killings'. Violent sex murders, some were found, some weren't. His daughter was never found. Say it damn near deranged him. Needless to say, the creoles again blamed the curse of the maloya woman."

"Why did they connect the killings?"

De Vries walked to the desk and produced a chiselled leather folder. He spilled a slew of assorted press cuttings from the 'Le Quotidien de La Réunion' on the table.

"There was always a red flower left at the scene. Sometimes real, sometimes etched in the victim's back or thigh. The hindus use the red flower as the symbol of the goddess Kali, when they sacrifice a chicken or a goat.

"When I went to the Legion, the finger was even pointed at me. But the killings continued after I had left. There have been none for three years now. But nobody's been caught, either. The killer's still out there. Somewhere." De Vries gestured towards the grey rocky outcrop on the horizon.

"Probably one of those interbred 'petits blancs' hillbillies, up on the plateau."

Tom Black stood up, and faced the volcano. "Kali and *le volcan*," he said. "I'm getting to know the ghosts that haunt this place."

De Vries continued, facing the window with his back to Black. "Now, de C has his ideas about how to expand in the cane business. Most of them involve making trouble for us. It's all behind the scenes, nothing we can pin down. But since we laid off those fruit pickers, suddenly the workers in the sugar factory want a union. After 200 years. That's de C's work. To get into office on La Réunion, you need a coalition of the centre and 'les communistes'. Now, the communists are fighting us on worker's rights."

Black scowled and turned his glass in his hand. De Vries read his mind and laughed aloud. "My friend, I know what you are thinking. In the Legion, we would simply have knocked the fight out of them with a thirty-mile hike. Well, out here in the real world, there is no blind obedience. A pity, I know. Welcome back to democracy!" said de Vries.

"There's a lot to be said for a few hours of 'pelote' with a pack of stones on your back," said Black, only half in jest. "When the situation calls for some ... attitude adjustment."

A ringing bell drifted over from another part of the house. A coloured maid with a bright print headband leaned around the door and excused herself. "Mr. Pouletain from the newspaper is on the line, sir. Again."

"Give us one minute, and then put him through, Marie," said de Vries.

"Pouletain's a good guy, Tom. You should meet him. He's going to be pumping me about the casino, probably about the union thing too. But he knows what a '*salaud*' de C is, and he's been fair to us in the past."

De Vries replenished Black's glass. As he placed the decanter back on the baize table, the telephone on his desk began to ring.

"Paul, how are you. Before you say a word, I have nothing yet on the fire. I need to speak to Commissaire Delasalles first."

De Vries fell silent and listened intently. "If you think that's necessary. We can do that. Sure."

He hung up, and turned to Black. "Pouletain has something he doesn't want to talk about over the phone. Sometimes the operators at the exchange listen in. He wants me to meet him in 15 minutes in town. Do you feel up to it? You can take a nap instead, if you like."

De Vries was wearing a slight smirk. This was Tom Black, a man who had just spent 15 years in the toughest regiment on earth. If a legionnaire was lying down in the afternoon, he was already dead.

*****

La Réunion Upland: the previous night

Sheet lightning cut the angry sky as detective Marcel Terreblanche drew his police vehicle into the mud of a clearing near Takamaka, on the plateau between the volcanoes. The flash lit the features of the two officers with him in the car, Sergeant Emile Danceau and Gendarme Hono Sauvigny.

"I can't see a thing in this bloody rain," said Danceau, switching on his torch and training it on the shack nestling behind the small, overgrown garden.

"This is Branco's. I recognise that thing in the window," said Terreblanche. Danceau redirected his torch.

"You've been here before? You didn't mention it," Danceau said. The barb in the comment was not lost on Terreblanche. The mutual disdain of the two men was palpable. Danceau knew Terreblanche was on the payroll of the de Cs; Terreblanche knew Danceau was not, and he had to be careful.

"Branco must be a Christian. It's the Black Virgin of St. Marie." Another crack of lightning took a snapshot of the scene. At the side of the shack, the fern-like leaves of a fanjan tree flailed wildly, still battling with the tail-end of the cyclone.

Danceau held the torch over his watch. It was 12.42am.

They sprang from the car into the half-shelter provided by the small, raised verandah. A shirt in faded red cheesecloth, heavy with rain, was tangled in sodden disorder around the balustrade.

"We're looking for any flammables that might match those used at the St. Expedit Casino. Gasoline, paraffin, canisters, wadding. Sauvigny, check if that shirt is complete, or if it has been ripped up for rags," said Terreblanche.

Danceau placed an iron crowbar in the jamb of the door, which cracked easily under his weight. He flicked back the mosquito screen. Inside, the darkness was total, the only sound the rain, hammering like shelled peas on the roof.

Danceau pointed his torch and, starting on the left, slid the disk of light slowly over the room. Sauvigny cursed as a rivulet of water dripped from the roof, and trickled down his neck.

In the centre of the floor stood a stack of palettes that functioned as a makeshift table. On the patchwork tablecloth sat a giant clam shell, filled to the brim with beer bottle tops.

A gas heater in the corner served as a second, smaller table. On top stood a white ceramic washbowl and plate, with a faded pattern of dots in assorted colours. "My mother has one just the same," said Sauvigny, gauchely.

Terreblanche wiped the sweat from his brow and the back of his neck.

Danceau moved his light to the corners of the room. Behind the door stood a formless object that, at first, looked like an umbrella stand. As he moved closer, Danceau made out a collection of three hunting spears, standing upright in an old Slazenger golf bag.

Three-quarters of the floor was covered by a single piece of lino. Its pattern of faded brown squares was straight out of the 1960s.

Terreblanche closed the wall cupboard that served as a small pantry. "I can smell some kind of chemicals," he said.

Danceau fell into a kneeling position and moved the light along the base of the wall. Sauvigny lay on his stomach as the light swept under the small bed in the corner. He pulled out a pair of dirty white sports shoes, and a dog-eared soccer magazine.

"The chemicals smell is stronger here," he said to Terreblanche. "Maybe spilled on the lino or the floorboards."

Danceau and Terreblanche heaved together, lifting the wooden bedframe. Sauvigny hauled the lino out from under the bedlegs, turning it back on itself towards the middle of the floor.

"Paraffin. Smells like paraffin," said Sauvigny. The two more experienced cops did not answer.

"Lift the boards," said Danceau, handing over the iron bar.

The wood was soft as cork after the wet season. It yielded easily, offering no resistance to the lever.

The rain had grown more intense. The storm was almost overhead now. Another burst of sheet lightning picked out Sauvigny's face and lit the gaping hole where the now-vertical floorboard had been.

Sauvigny's hand froze on the rough wood.

"O Jesus Marie" he stammered. Then he fell backwards, gagging.

*****

At sixteen minutes past three, de Vries and Black pushed open the door of Domineo's Beach Bar in St. Pierre. Pouletain was already standing at the bar.

"Hello, Jacques, good to see you."

"Paul, let me get you a rum coffee."

Pouletain nodded gratefully. A journalist never says no to a coffee, or a rum. They lengthen the conversation.

"So," said de Vries, "How stands the nation?

"The nation, Jacques, seems to have gone crazy. Sorry to learn about the casino. I heard that, in the cyclone alert, the fire people could not attend."

Pouletain was clearly agitated. He would not wait for his drink, to say what he had to say. De Vries could see the alarm in his eyes.

"They brought in Branco and Cheron last night. You are probably aware."

"Yes. I have to go to Delasalles to find out if they got anything out of them. But if Branco was working for de C, we'll know soon enough – because he'll be back out on the street. By this afternoon he'll probably be over at Omar's, swilling beer and laughing at us.

"By the way Paul, this is Tom Black, my good friend from the Legion. He saved my life. He's come to work for us in the casinos."

"Monsieur," Pouletain nodded to Black, remembering that he

had forgotten his manners. He had the drawn look of a man who'd had a long night.

"Branco won't be swilling beers anywhere this afternoon, Jacques," said Pouletain.

"I just heard he died in police custody, during the night."

*****

Pouletain left the bar and went downtown, promising to meet them again in three hours, when he had more information.

He would speak to Danceau, not Terreblanche. Danceau would usually mark his card when something spicy was going on. Pouletain knew all about Danceau's personal collection of photographs of naked, mutilated women. He had stolen them from the station, during the Kali Killings. So Danceau was happy to help.

Back at the mansion, De Vries paced back and forth on the ornate Moroccan rug that was another memento of his African days.

"What the hell is de C up to. Either it was suicide, or it was murder. If it was murder, it couldn't happen without his say-so. Toto always says that de C's thugs are like the catfish down in the bay – dangerous only in shoals. But de C himself, he's like the scorpion fish. He'll come at you on his own," said de Vries.

Black shrugged his shoulders. "Let's assume he did hire Branco to lay the fire. Once he was identified and arrested, de C wanted him silenced. Does it have to be more complicated than that?"

"I don't think he'd go that far," said de Vries. "He'd be arrogant enough to think he's untouchable, and anyway, Branco could never talk – not if he wants to live on La Réunion."

Black nodded. "Come to think of it, nobody's mentioned the other one – what was his name? Cheron. De C would have had to silence both."

The door opened. De Vries senior entered, a stocky man with a shock of white hair and the bearing of a major general. He was clutching a crumpled telegram.

"Ah, Monsieur Black. I'm sorry I was not here to meet you. We have been busy, between acts of God, and acts of men. Under the circumstances, you will understand." It was not a question, and Tom Black did not reply.

He held up the yellowed sheet. "It appears we will be covered by the insurance, especially since they have made a capture. So far so good."

He turned again to Black. "Please accept my assurance that life at Savannah is not usually so ... shall we say ... diverting."

"I'm sure it is not, Mr. de Vries."

"Please, call me Emil." He picked up an oriental scrimshaw casket from a bookshelf, and flipped back the lid.

"Davidoff, Black. Those damn Cubans might be killing my sugar business with their cheap exports, but they still make the best damn cigar in the world." Both Tom and de Vries picked out a cigar, and began the ritual of paring them.

"Papa, Branco is dead. They found him this morning. In the police cells," said de Vries.

Emil de Vries did not look up, but the hand holding the lighter froze an inch from the cigar. His brow furrowed slightly, before he proceeded.

"Le petit de C never fails to impress me, Monsieur Black," he said.

"We have a man accused of burning down my casino, with no known connections to the de Cs, turning up dead, with just four months to go before the election. Where will the blame be laid? At this house." De Vries pointed at the floor with his cigar, to emphasise his point.

"The truth is of little import. The publicity alone will turn the neutral vote against me."

De Vries looked at his father. "Pouletain is digging around to see what he can get. He knows which stones to turn over. We meet him in an hour at the beach."

Emil de Vries was not listening. "This is going to suit the communists down to the ground. That imbecile Volontère is already baying for my blood over the sugar union. We'll have to tread carefully on this. It's election year at the Ministry in Paris, too, and they've been looking for an excuse to pull back our sugar subsidy. It won't help if La Réunion looks like a den of squabbling cats."

*****

Black and de Vries were in Domineo's Beach Bar for twenty minutes, before Pouletain brushed through the door. He had looked nervous during their first meeting, but he was positively ashen-faced now.

The bar was dark and empty, save for a couple of barflies at the front. They had chosen a booth in the corner, for privacy. Pulling back a chair, Pouletain nodded to the barman and said "Hold the coffee this time. Just bring the rum."

When the glass was set before him, he rifled it in one. "Gentlemen, I would advise you to partake of a rum punch. You are going to need it."

De Vries held up three fingers. The drinks were brought. Pouletain waited until the barman was back out of earshot.

"When Branco was brought in last night, they got a warrant and went up to the plateau to search his shack. They took up the floorboards and found a whole lot of weird voodoo stuff – knives and billhooks, also goat skulls, and the mummified body of a hyena.

"They also found the partially decomposed corpses of three human females, treated to preserve them as far as is possible in this heat."

De Vries lowered his glass. "Are you telling me..."

"What I'm telling you, Jacques, is that it looks like they caught the Kali Killer."

Pouletain flipped open a black pocket notebook, and thumbed to the details of his conversation with Danceau.

"Two white women and one Indian. They reckon one of the whites is that Australian tourist who disappeared while swimming near La Possession. Body never found. They assumed she'd been washed out to sea.

"The red flowers on the other corpses were to direct suspicion towards the malabars, or the other hindus. With these three, as well as preserving the corpses, he left jewellery in place. One had a necklace that was identified. It belonged to Lisette de C."

De Vries was struggling to take it all in. Like most of them, he had been fooled by the red flowers into thinking the killer had to be a non-white.

"So what happened at police HQ last night? Did Branco find some way to kill himself?" said de Vries.

"Far from it. When de C heard they had found Lisette, he ordered that Branco be released into his personal custody, and sent a car. That was the last they saw of him alive."

"Is Branco's body at the gendarmerie?"

"Yes. The body was brought back to the station at dawn. The driver needed help when he brought it in – for shock, I mean. Danceau said de C had Branco tied to a chair in one of the outhouses on his estate. Left the house with a steam iron and a pair of pliers, and did a medieval number on him. They said the screaming went on for three hours. They're going to depend on blood and fingerprints to identify the corpse. Teeth are gone, his balls have been torn off, and the face and most of the body skin burned away."

If they hadn't seen worse in the Legion, de Vries and Black might have turned pale.

"If it's true, de C is finished," said Black. "And not just in politics. In business as well."

He drained his glass, looked at it for a second, and held it up towards the bar.

De Vries was beginning to see the positive side. "*Allons, mes copains.* This is the end of the road for Monsieur de C.

"I'm afraid Paris will insist."

8

LA RÉUNION, FOUR MONTHS LATER

The stream of blood running from Tom Black's lips did not bother him as much as the rip under the arm of his best suit.

He was standing at the window of the office over the de Vries casino, his arm above his head like a classical Greek statue.

He had ruined his jacket ejecting an angry customer who had pawned his mistress' jewellery and lost the money at the poker table.

Normally, Black would have walked away, leaving his doormen to deal with it. A gentleman, after all, is one who can play the clarinet, but does not.

But this guy had sliced up the baize of an antique gaming table with a small, ivory-handled stiletto, and then done the same to the doorman's face.

The face could be repaired. The card table, however, had come from de Vries house, and had sentimental value.

Besides, knives weren't allowed in Tom Black's casinos. Now the guy had a busted jaw to prove it.

"When he tell his woman about her jewellery, that jaw ain't goin' to be his biggest problem," said Toto, grinning.

Toto handed Black a paper tissue, and took a seat by the door.

He produced a small brown object from a paper bag in his side pocket, and crunched it between his teeth. The object was a 'moon biscuit', produced once a year by the local Chinese for their annual festival. Outside the window, the first firecrackers were already livening up the early evening in St. Pierre.

It was late September. The 'Festival of the Dead' had begun.

*****

Fifteen minutes later, Black and Toto settled into a booth in the bar, opposite Jacques de Vries and Marcel Pouletain.

Rum coffees were brought. Toto was working on his third moon biscuit.

Two garish, bug-eyed paper dragons bedecked the canopy over the bar, further trappings of the Festival of the Dead. The staccato tones of Chinese music echoed over the tannoy.

"Marcel thinks he knows the real reason why Cerque and the Communists won't line out with us in the general election," said de Vries. He turned his coffee cup slowly on the saucer. He was looking stressed. The pressure of organising his father's electoral campaign was taking its toll.

"The good news is that it's not personal," said Pouletain, checking a small silver pocket watch that he had pulled from his waistcoat pocket.

"The communists need you as much as you need them. They're glad to be shot of de C, and your father is known to be fair and clean. But let's face it. The cane business is a low-wage business that's been on the ropes since the Cubans started exporting again. Only the French subsidy keeps it going. But Cerque can't see the reasons for the low wages. He just sees exploitation. He thinks that to align his party with you would be political suicide."

"Knowing his grass roots, he's probably right," said de Vries, stretching his arms and rubbing his eyes.

"The cane business is in my father's bones. In mine, too. Besides, nobody's going to buy into sugar these days. What is the way forward?"

Black was only half-listening. He was staring at the mirror between the two men, examining his reflection. The lip had stopped bleeding, but he had taken a fairly competent left hook from the poker player. His right eye was already puffy.

He would be pretty in the morning.

*****

Half an hour later, Black and Toto emerged into the cool air and walked to Toto's jeep.

Toto did not normally offer to drive Tom Black. When he did, Black knew he had something on his mind.

The road, from St. Pierre back to Savannah, would be their chance to have a word alone.

De Vries had stayed on at the casino. He would have four more beers with Pouletain, before the night was out. Seven months home from Africa, but the dust of the Legion still lay coarse and dry in his throat.

"Old Monsieur de Vries had some visitors at Savannah a few weeks before Jacques came home last spring," said Toto.

"As far as I know, he didn't tell Jacques about them. Even Pouletain doesn't know, and he keeps tabs on everyone who comes to La Réunion. Me, I just kept my mouth shut. Until now."

Black shifted in his seat to turn towards Toto. "What kind of visitors?"

A distant firecracker split the darkness, as the lights of St. Pierre filled the rear view mirror. They passed the last streetlight, and nosed out on to the coast road to St. Joseph.

"Couple of guys came over from Cape Town. Interested in purchasing de Vries lands in Madagascar for some kind of tourist park. Of course, de Vries don't see it as land, he sees it as sugar plantation. Maybe they should have told him they were buying into the sugar business. That way, he might have listened to them."

"I take it he turned them down?"

"Flat. Those two gentlemen walked out with their rolls of maps, looking like two whipped dogs."

Toto allowed himself a chuckle, then suddenly was deadly serious again.

"I saw 'em sign the visitor's book at Savannah, when they came in. If you want to get their names."

*****

In a room full of creole Chinese in ceremonial costume, finding a tall Frenchman named Thierry Lefargue had not been difficult.

Besides, he had his name badge on his lapel.

He had been standing with his secretary at the front of the suite rented by the 'Ligue Communiste Revolutionnaire de la Réunion' for the occasion. They held a Festival of the Dead party every year. In a multi-coloured colony, it made sense to court each ethnic group.

The stranger had introduced himself as a tv director, researching a documentary for France 1 on politics in the country's largest dependency.

Lefargue was fourth in line in the Ligue, after Jojo Lamarre, Marie Blenois and Cerque himself. But he felt he should be third, and had jumped at the chance of a photo opportunity, especially one on a national network.

They had withdrawn to a dark corner of the hotel bar to talk. Lefargue lit a slim panatella and took the first sip of his fourth whiskey. It tasted better than the last. He was tipsy, talkative. Normally he would have unbuttoned his collar, pulled down his tie. But this was a tv guy, and, if you wanted to wind up on film, appearances were important.

He looked at the director's business card. Serge Noir, L.L.D., Productions Domino, 16, rue des Citronniers, 75756 Paris CEDEX 12.

"We'll be looking at the communist party of the future on La Réunion. Trying to identify the potential successors to Monsieur Cerque," said Noir.

"Besides you and the other three officers, there is of course, as an outsider perhaps, young Martineau."

"Martineau," said Lefargue, drawing on his panatella. "Martineau has enthusiasm. But he also has his damn idealism. He's all theory. No notion of *realpolitik*. Too much Marx. And not enough ... Spencer."

He sniggered through a haze of blue smoke, visibly pleased with his attempt at levity. This was his chance to move around the hive like a newborn queen bee, stinging the other queens to death.

"And Marie Blenois?"

Lefargue shook his head. "Blenois isn't a runner. The party here is less modern than on the mainland. Not ready for a female leader yet. Besides, she lacks the hard edge. She'd have us holding coffee mornings. It's the wrong image for the party of 1917." He never missed a chance to put a knife in the back of the woman keeping him in fourth place.

Noir stared thoughtfully at the burnished red liquid in his tumbler. "That leaves just you and Jojo Lamarre. Your party needs a partner in the centre, though, to have 'critical mass' in Paris. Lamarre has held back in criticising the other parties, while you have been, let's say, more vocal. How do you think de Vries and his party would view you? You've roasted him for his interests in the sugar business."

Lefargue frowned. Noir's words were chosen carefully, but the truth was still hurting.

He took another slug of whiskey, without noticing that Noir had hardly touched his own. He placed his glass gingerly on the table, with the over-cautious manner of a man on his second half-bottle.

"Listen, Noir. His sugar interests are what make de V our perfect ally. They are his Achilles' heel. On the one hand, he needs our help every year to lobby for the subsidy. On the other, sugar makes him vulnerable. All one needs do is mention wage structures. Believe me, Noir, Cerque is delighted to have a presidential candidate who would be so easy to control."

Noir smiled and finished scribbling notes in his black leatherbound pad. He seemed to have all he needed to know.

The door burst open and the chinese waiter sailed through from the function room. For the Festival, he was wearing a red silk tunic. He looked like the young Chairman Mao.

Noir raised his glass in the direction of the billowing cloud around Lefargue.

"Aux morts," he said. "To the dead. Santé!"

*****

Through the narrow side panel of the yacht, Tom Black looked over to Cape Town and the rugged outline of Table Mountain beyond.

The yacht was the Lydia, named for the youngest daughter of Geoffrey Morgenstern, the man seated across the cabin facing him. He was the president of MS Leisure Corporation, South Africa's third-largest tourism development company, and its leading hotel developer.

The bespectacled, bookish man behind Morgenstern was his finance director, Tom Wilson. Together they were the 'whipped dogs' Toto had seen at Savannah, calling to see old man de Vries.

In front of the three men stood Dr. Zandra Singh, associate professor of the Institute of Zoology at Rhodes University, and advisor to Morgenstern Leisure. They listened intently as she concluded her presentation on the lemurs of Antsalova, Western Madagascar.

"These lemuridae are the oldest surviving ancestors of the modern monkey. All four of these species: the ring-tailed, the ruffed, the crown and the black lemur, are now recognised as 'endangered' by the World Wildlife Organisation.

"All four are to be found primarily in Antsalova, and in the more northern parts of Madagascar, precisely where the de Vries Corporation has its lands. This is why I believe a properly maintained and protected wildlife park, such as Mr. Morgenstern proposes, is crucial to their survival."

Morgenstern turned, nodding his appreciation to Zandra Singh and spreading his hands expansively in the air. "So, Mr. Black. You will understand our disappointment that Mr. de Vries does not share our vision. In fact, as he put it, he does not want his beloved cane plantations turned into a 'monkey park'."

Tom Black did not smile. He could tell that Morgenstern, for his light tone, did not regard the situation as frivolous. An investment of a large fortune in a tourism resort built around a national park was not a frivolous matter.

Morgenstern continued.

"If I may be candid with you, Mr. Black, the Madagascar authorities had told us to expect as much from Mr. de Vries. However, while our interest is primarily a commercial one, we also have their support, and that of Dr. Singh and the Institute, from an environmental point of view. In time, Mr. de Vries, as a public figure, could find himself under considerable pressure.

"Which makes us all the more pleased to see you here. Am I to understand that you believe he could be persuaded to assist us?"

Black smiled. "I would say that other considerations have emerged that could influence him to sell ... if we can structure a reasonable deal, of course."

He thought of Toto's promise to him before he left. "You talk to the Morgensterns and in the meanwhile, leave Mr. de Vries to me. I know something that might just bring the old man round."

Black looked directly at Morgenstern. It was time to test the waters. "Gentlemen, let us be under no illusions. These are large tracts of natural habitat, but also prime commercial land. De Vries can only sell these waterlands once, and he will demand a commercial price. We have to be talking hundreds of millions."

"Rand." Wilson's flat, cold accountant's voice butted hastily into the conversation.

"Dollars." said Black without flinching.

He looked away towards Table Mountain, to allow his words to sink in. The hard, naked shoulder of rock reminded him of Ben Bulben, back in Ireland.

He thought of Drumcliff Churchyard at Ben Bulben's foot, and the plain grey headstone of Yeats within. Morgenstern shifted uneasily in his seat as the two calculated the financial implications of the demand.

Black sat in silence. To hold his nerve, he visualised Yeats' epitaph on the cold limestone:

> *"Cast a cold eye*
> *On life, on death.*
> *Horseman, pass by."*

*****

Just after 9pm that evening, Tom Black emerged from the cable car at the top of Table Mountain and walked to the restaurant above the cable station.

The cool air atop the mountain would help him unwind, after the pressure of the meeting with Morgenstern and Wilson.

From the call booth he dialled Savannah. Camps Bay and the city glowed in the dusk far below. There was a click, a short delay, and then the distant voice of Jacques de Vries. He was indistinct, crackling, but it was good to hear a friend.

"Jacques ... it went well. They are still interested. I think there is a prospect of a deal."

"Time is running out, Tom." De Vries was keening, like an echo in an underground tunnel.

"My flight gets in tomorrow evening at 6.10pm. We'll talk then," said Black.

Outside in the fresh air again, he looked over the city and the Cape flats. Now it was up to Toto, to change the old man's mind.

There was nothing more Black could do tonight. He would take the next car down the mountain, have dinner and a bottle of Meerlust Rubicon at his hotel, and be in bed by midnight.

*****

The creole voice on Radio Freedom crackled over the apron of the airfield at St. Denis. "First of October, but temperatures still in the high thirties. Cyclone probability low."

Jacques de Vries mopped his brow with a handkerchief, as Tom Black stepped briskly down the airplane gangway, and jogged on to the baking tarmac.

Through the tinted glass of the terminal building, De Vries could see Manto, the baggage handler, sipping coffee in the cafeteria. The bags would not be out for ten minutes yet. He led Black round the front of the plane. They would take a short stroll.

"I tried to talk to my father again last night. He's stubborn as that volcano," said de Vries, gesturing towards the uplands behind the airstrip. He took on his father's clipped, husky voice. "If there was no sugar, the people would have no work. If they had no work, they would have to take welfare. It's better for Paris to send the money as a sugar subsidy. At least that way, the people keep their self-respect."

"Maybe he's got a point. But now, it's all down to Toto," answered Black.

"What do you mean?" said de Vries. Toto's plan was news to him.

"He said he might have an ace to play."

De Vries looked thoughtful. "Well, Toto and our family go back a long way. Toto's grandfather was a slave on our plantations. We didn't get around to abolishing slavery here until 1848."

Black looked up to the mountains decked with sugar cane. He had dark shadows under his eyes. The strain of the last few days was beginning to show.

"So what's the news from Cape Town?" said de Vries.

"Morgenstern wouldn't go for a straight cash deal. He's offered a cash and assets split. For the sugarlands in Madagascar and Réunion, De Vries Holdings would realise $43m, plus two four-star hotels owned by Morgenstern Leisure in Cape Town. Most of the sugar workers could probably be absorbed into the leisure group, so unemployment would be minimal. Perhaps that will help convince your father."

"Nearly half of our workers are casual anyway. They come over from Madagascar just for harvest time," said de Vries. "As for the figures, they sound ok. We can always haggle later."

"There's one more thing I'll be telling your father tomorrow," said Black. He had stopped, and turned to face de Vries.

"If I manage to broker the deal, I want to be brought inside. As a director, not an employee."

De Vries was stony-faced. He paused for a full twenty seconds. He had not been fixed by the cold blue of Black's gaze since they had left the Legion.

Then he smiled. "Damn hot for September."

De Vries turned, and took Black by the arm. "Look, *I* won't object. But you'll have to get that one past the old man yourself. And sooner you than me."

Black looked back to the plane. Manto had started hauling the bags from the aircraft's open underbelly on to a rickety cargo trolley.

"Yes," said Black.

"Damn hot for September."

*****

At 12.30pm the next day, de Vries was on his knees under a photocopier in the electoral office in St. Pierre.

Red and blue ribands decked the white walls. A five-foot high 'V' logo with his father's picture as its centrepiece dominated the back wall. It looked like a presidential election in Washington DC.

He clicked the steel door of the Xerox machine into place and pressed the switch. The machine shuddered into life, and began spitting yellow fliers neatly into the tray.

A worried-looking brunette was standing over him in a white blouse and plaid business skirt. The matching jacket was draped over a chair at the back of the room. The newspaper she was holding showed a cartoon of de Vries senior as a pirate. He stood at the helm of a galleon, a patch over one eye and a patterned bandana on his head.

"It's not good, Jacques. He's too easy to attack. It's the same old song: pillaging the island, robbing the poor of a decent wage. Not good, with the elections three months away."

"I know, Marilyn, but all we can do is fight fires. Maybe we should issue a flier to say 'Work is better than welfare'".

He did not see her cringe at his suggestion. The door almost left its hinges as Toto and Black came barrelling in, with two large green bottles on their arms. Black was clearly ecstatic. He was brandishing the same newspaper.

"Jacques, the pirate's buccaneering days are over. He accepted Morgenstern's offer. I faxed the o.k. to Cape Town half an hour ago."

There was a loud crack as the first of the champagne corks sailed up to the roof. Toto began handing out paper cups.

"I would have called, but I wanted to tell you in person," said Black.

"Here's to De Vries *Leisure* Corporation, and goodbye to De Vries Sugar. Jacques, it's a great day for the Madagascar monkey!"

In an instant, gloom had turned to celebration. Jacques de Vries was having trouble keeping up. "This champagne tastes like fish oil," was all he could manage.

He thought he had better catch up on the introductions. "Tom, Marilyn here is our new PR woman and office manager. You can speak freely with her around. So! Tell us about the meeting you had with my father, at Savannah."

"Well, I think we all can take credit for bringing him around. It would appear the idea grew on him, even while he was resisting it. As they say, nothing's more powerful than an idea whose time has come, eh, Toto?"

It was Toto's cue to explain what he had done. "Look at you two, grinning like a couple of scorpion fish. Well, you boys make one mistake when you talk to Mr. de Vries. He's never lived anywhere else but this island. He might be a '*z'Oreils*' white planter – but he thinks like a creole. And when we creole thinkin', we don't look for some high-price advisor; we look for omens in the sky, in the air, on the land. He needed an omen he ain't never seen before. So yesterday, he see his first *endormi*."

De Vries put down his cup. "The endormi. Hell, even I've never seen one. But then that's his business, the endormi – not being seen," said de Vries.

"I saw a picture of one once," said Marilyn, whose head was already filling with bubbles of cheap champagne.

Black was looking confused.

"The endormi chameleon, Tom," said de Vries. He took on a mock Irish accent: "Rarest *baist* in all of La Réunion."

Toto took up his story again.

"I know a spot near the River of Rocks where you can find that old endormi, and we got lucky," he said. "Made it look like an omen to your daddy. I tells him the message the endormi had for him: sometimes you changes your colours a little to survive," said Toto, in a reverent tone.

"You change your colours, but you still the same, underneath. You could have sat Mr. de V in every fancy bank from here to Port Louis. All them pretty-boy advisors wouldn't have made no difference to him. But yesterday his eyes nearly popped. He'd never seen that old endormi."

"That *oooold* endormi," said Marilyn, tilting her cup to Toto and sniggering.

*****

An hour later, de Vries drained the last drops of champagne from his paper cup. Toto had set off back to Savannah. Marilyn had taken the afternoon off. De Vries and Black were alone in the office.

Black placed the telephone receiver back in its hook. He had notified Morgenstern he would fly to Cape Town with the de Vries's the following day. It was Wednesday. With luck, the heads of agreement could be signed over the weekend.

De Vries had recovered from his initial bafflement. "I'm glad the old man finally saw sense. Paris won't keep the sugar subsidy forever. We had ten years at most, before the sugar interests started to bleed money. They might have pulled the whole export business – fruit, vanilla, coffee – down with them.

"Underneath, he just wouldn't see his workers losing their jobs. I don't think this is down to any damn chameleon, no disrespect to Toto. My bet is: he bought it when he heard they'd all find work in the casinos and the hotels."

Black was rummaging in his pocket. He tossed a piece of purple card on to the desk, just where de Vries, lounging back in his chair, had propped his heels. "There's something else. I had an omen lined up for him myself."

De Vries picked up the card. "Who the hell is Serge Noir?"

"Just a nobody I dreamed up to get to Lefargue. Told him I was a tv guy, doing a documentary. Lefargue told me your sugar companies gave the communists an easy advantage. When they needed to twist your arm, they'd roll out the wages issue. I don't think your father had been able to admit that to himself. He had his head buried in the sand. Until this morning. But I had to get it from source – from Cerque or Lefargue themselves," said Black.

"Black, you are a scheming bastard," said de Vries, shaking his head. "I'm glad we've got you on our side."

Black laughed. "That's almost exactly what your father said this morning, when he made me a director. Fifteen year contract."

"Now that does give us something to celebrate," said de Vries.

"So. What's this phoney qualification you've given yourself here – L.L.D.?"

Black looked out at St. Pierre, and the streets that, for the next fifteen years at least, were going to be his home.

"It's a special diploma from Ireland. Very popular with our lads who've emigrated to the States. Stands for 'Lately Left Donegal'".

9

DONEGAL, IRELAND, NOVEMBER 2004

Hobo leaned against the wall, the last button on his threadbare tweed jacket tapping the window in the wind. In the puddle where he stood, the reflection showed muddied boots, and breeches piled in crumpled disorder above them. His tongue half-protruded as he peered through the window into the lobby.

He was watching the stranger who had entered the hotel a minute before.

It was a mid-morning in late November. The tourists had departed, the season was over, and the lobby of the Mulroy Bay Hotel was quiet.

Matt Heneghan stood at the bar, unaware of the watcher outside. He turned over the coins in his pocket, and listened to the hollow grumble of a kettle rising to the boil, somewhere under the bar counter. The road from Dublin had been longer than he had remembered.

He squinted at the clutch of whiskey bottles under the mirror, and whispered a familiar poetry: Jameson, Bushmills, Tullamore, Power. The kettle's crescendo lured the barman out of the shadows. "I'll take the Jameson," said Heneghan.

He looked on as the red liquid swirled together with the boiling water, sugar, lemon and cloves. He carried the glass to a circular mahogany table in the corner, and settled into a leather armchair, under the leafy canopy of an umbrella plant.

The fireplace was stocked with rough-hewn blocks of wood, but they were not alight.

To the right of the bar, a pair of eyes peering through round spectacles loomed up behind the glass of the reception office, between the postcards and the taxi notices. The hotel manageress, Miss McGarrigle, had not seen the man with the Dublin-registered car in Carrigart before.

Heneghan unfurled the August issue of "Business Plus" magazine, and looked at the picture on the cover. A smiling, tanned man in a dinner suit was thowing a pair of red dice across a casino gaming table. 'Betting on Black' was written in old-fashioned serif letters that matched the roulette wheel.

Tom Black's plans for fifteen years on La Réunion had turned into almost twice that, and now he was coming home. After five decades in the tropical sun, the kindly photo artist had been good enough to smooth the worst crow's feet from the weathered, still-handsome face.

Over the article inside, the headline ran: 'The Prodigal Son Returns. Tom Black talks to Tony Dwyer about building a gambling empire in the Indian Ocean'. In a second photo, Black was standing by a shiny Daimler, resplendent in the formal dress uniform of the Foreign Legion.

Outside the Mulroy Bay Hotel, a wet wind was roaring. The hot whiskey warmed Heneghan, and the sweet fragrance of the cloves filled his head.

He settled down to read the report again.

*****

Tom Black had taken the call six days ago.

He had been working at the offices of 'Fondation Noir' in Paris, the working title of the *Association d'Amitié Franco-Irlandaise* he had founded in 1987 to build cultural and human relations between Ireland and France.

Heneghan had said only that he was from the Department of Foreign Affairs, and had been given Black's name by a contact at the United Nations. He wanted to meet in Donegal.

Black had rolled his eyes at the cloak and dagger, but the mention of the UN intrigued him and he was vain enough to want to know more. He would be in Donegal in any case, meeting a shipment of antiques and art from La Réunion. Provided, that is, that the forty-foot truck could negotiate Bunlin Bridge, the narrow river crossing at his new estate between Milford and Carrigart.

He had agreed to the meeting, and his Lear jet had slipped into Carrickfin Airport late the previous night.

The blue metallic Chrysler jeep swept through the rain, and pulled up at the Mulroy Bay Hotel. The old hobo, still leaning at the window, turned and thrust his hands deep into his pockets. He lurched away with the purposeful stride of a man with his own inscrutable plan. Long before he had turned the corner, he seemed to fade into the drizzle that was drifting in from the bay.

Heneghan had sounded genuine on the phone. Nonetheless, Black had opted to meet him in public, rather than at the house. Now, his head filling with the bleakness and purity of Donegal, he wondered if he had been overly suspicious.

Heneghan's soft, clipped accent told Black that he was from the midlands, perhaps Laois or Athlone, but had been living in Dublin for years. Somewhere south of the Liffey, he guessed. One of the better areas.

As Black shook his hand and sat down, Heneghan tapped on the open magazine.

"Director of De Vries Holdings, also Chairman since the death of Emile de Vries in 1982. Landmark deals with tour operators, notably to offer gambling holidays for the new wealthy from Russia and Central Asia. Deals that quadrupled the group's value in the first ten years alone. Set up Fondation Noir, in 1989 appointed to the board of Banque Franco-Irlandaise."

He did not mention the article's claim that Black was worth £80 million.

"So. Have you come home to put your feet up, Tom?"

The waiter brought two hot whiskeys, and lifted a box of matches from behind a vase in the fireplace. He busied himself with the fire. In the office window, Miss McGarrigle appeared again between the postcards. This older man she had seen before. He was the new one, she noted with some satisfaction, who had bought land out the road.

"I'm not so sure I'm home, Matt. I've built the house, all right. But where I now live? I'd have to think about that one."

"Let me tell you why I'm here, Tom. Why I'm taking up your time. And thanks for meeting me, by the way. The Taoiseach is in Donegal tomorrow. He's opening a new factory over in Gweedore, some German crowd making motor components. While he's up here, he'd like to meet you."

The wood crackled and spat in the grate, as if casting doubt on Heneghan's words. Black joined his hands in a prayerful motion, and touched them to his lips.

"You mentioned the U.N. Is this something to do with the U.N.?"

"Not exactly. I'd as soon let him talk to you himself. I mentioned the U.N. because our senior woman there praised the work your foundation does for children. You remember Evelyn de Burca."

The name took Black by surprise. He had slammed the phone down on Evelyn de Burca when a grant assessment of one of his projects, led by Foreign Affairs, had run over schedule. The praise was coming from an unexpected quarter.

"Evelyn's an impressive woman. Funny, I thought I'd rubbed her the wrong way."

"Not a bit of it. She was impressed by your ... by your drive," said Heneghan.

"That's very diplomatic. She was annoyed by my impatience. At times, it borders on the brusque."

Heneghan allowed himself a smile. "She did mention that you, well, like to get things done."

"That's even more diplomatic. She meant I can tell people where to get off in four languages."

Heneghan allowed himself a smile.

"Well, the Taoiseach seemed impressed by what he heard. For now, all I need is to give Dublin your o.k. to meet him tomorrow. An informal chat, in private. Away from Dublin and all the media attention."

Black nodded. "Fine. But I can't promise anything. Especially if Foley wants something from the French."

As they stepped outside and walked to their cars, he wondered what he, or the French, had to offer the prime minister of Ireland. He would have to call to Gallagher's shop to buy a paper.

*****

Tom Black stared out of the back window of the house at the Sikorsky helicopter standing in the grounds.

Taoiseach James Foley leaned on Michael Heneghan's outstretched arm. He stepped on to the soft soil of Black's unplanted garden, and strode briskly across to where Black himself stood, at the back entrance to the house.

Heneghan greeted Black somewhat formally, and took care of introductions. The helicopter pilot and a fourth man, whom Black took to be special branch, remained by the aircraft. The pilot lit up a cigarette, and strolled towards the trees.

"Taoiseach, I must apologise for the disorder here," said Black, "the house is just finished. In fact, some of the upper rooms still need a lick of paint."

They climbed a short flight of stairs into the main hall. Packing crates from the Réunion shipment populated the hallway, most of them still unopened. The floor was littered with wood-wool. Several paintings in ornate gold and ochre frames stood on the stone tiles, against the wall.

A fire was already roaring in the lounge. Above it, the mantelpiece was crowded with photographs of the previous twenty-nine years, the faces of de Vries and Toto prominent throughout. None had yet been hanged in its final position.

Black offered Heneghan and Foley the red leather sofa, and dusted off the armchair to take a place beside them. On an ebony coffee table stood a small silver tray with three white porcelain cups. He poured coffee from a thermos canister and offered milk. Then he sat back, and waited for Foley to speak.

"Tom, Matt here has told you that we need your help. It's a particular affair of state. Now, I'm sorry he wasn't able to tell you more, but as you will see, it's a delicate matter. I wanted to talk to you about it myself." He took a sip of coffee, to allow Black to digest his opening words.

Black looked at him over his cup. "Does this have to do with relations with France? I have to tell you, I've always preferred to bypass the politicians. Never had much time for the red tape. Consequently, I'm not so well connected in Paris."

"You're not so well connected in Ireland, either. That's why you're the perfect man to help us. To all intents and purposes, you're an unknown quantity." Years of speechifying on the 'chicken dinner' circuit had given the Taoiseach a tendency towards cliché.

"With no connections, I have no power."

"Wrong, Tom. With no connections, you have no enemies."

Black smiled. He had as many enemies as the next man. They were on an archipelago in the Indian Ocean, that was all. He let the thought drift. Foley continued.

"You've been away for so long. Like you were airbrushed out of history. Do you see what I'm getting at? You're not tainted, in the eyes of any particular camp here. A Derryman in Donegal, you can be either Irish or British. If it suits, you even have the French passport too.You've come from the business world, but you've been involved in politics. Then there's Foundation Noir. You've become a kind of unofficial statesman."

Black ignored the mispronounciation of 'Fondation'. He was wondering if Foley's man in Paris had been caught with his pants down. There had been nothing in the paper.

He gave his best 'puzzled' look. He needed a bottom line. Foley read his mind.

"It's the Good Friday Agreement, Tom. The peace process. You don't have to be Henry Kissinger, to see it's on the rocks. I need an icebreaker. Someone to operate in midfield, work behind the scenes. The mechanism has seized, and we need to get some movement. A floating negotiator might just get us the breakthrough we need."

Foley leaned forward, and slipped into a concerned, confiding tone. "The parties are putting on a brave face, Tom. But let's just say that not all the protagonists in this are visible on-stage. More to the point, not everyone is interested in seeing it work."

No wonder he wanted to keep this discussion private. *The papers would think it was Christmas,* Black thought. However, he would not over-react.

"I'd have to think about it. It's not the kind of thing I had in my life plan. As I say, politics is not my field."

Foley put on the frown he reserved for angry constituents: *I understand your concern.* "Not politics, Tom. In fact, you'd be as anonymous as we can keep you. A better word would be 'statesmanship'."

And perhaps, in closing, a gentle appeal to Black's ego. "You'd be an unofficial senator of the state."

Foley leaned back, indicating that their conversation was coming to an end.

"Look, Matt is up here until the weekend. He'll be around, if you want to talk. Think about it for a few days."

"My thinking might disappoint you, Taoiseach," said Black. The sudden use of the title brought a more formal note to the conversation.

Foley seemed not to hear. He was checking his watch. Suddenly, he was the affable, easy-going, rural Irishman. "I must get on, Tom. Question time in the Dail in two hours. Have a think about that for me, willya?"

Black nodded, as Foley pressed his hand. They moved towards the door and into the hall. The bodyguard and the pilot were standing below the doorstep, already stepping their cigarettes into the gravel.

Foley rubbed his hands, patted Black on the arm. He pointed to a clump of trees a quarter of a mile away, on the Milford side. "That's Cratlagh Wood. Site of the the famous Leitrim murder. I have relations up the road here, Tom. The McCabe's of Carrigart. Cousins of my mother's."

Black nodded again. "When I meet them, I'll say hello." The four moved off towards the helicopter.

The Sikorsky's nose dipped, and it rose over the trees. Foley gave a cheery wave through the small window. The blue shape banked east to avoid the forest top, then curved towards Milford and headed south.

Inside the helicopter, Foley pulled on his headphones and pressed his microphone to his chin. Heneghan raised his eyebrows, enquiring Foley felt the meeting had gone.

"Hard to say. We'll drop you now in Milford. You hang around for a few days and keep working on him. I'm counting on him needing something to do. Donegal can be a lonely enough place. They accept you in their own time."

Watching from the ground, Black wondered how discreet a visit could be, in a seven-ton chopper that could be heard for miles around. He stepped inside, and leaned back against the heavy oak door.

At least he didn't give me the 'do it for your country' line.

He fished in his pocket for his car keys. It was time to see if Gallagher had a decent bottle of Scotch.

10

South Wales, Gower Peninsula, Autumn 2004

Sir Anthony Cathcart was nervous.

With a crunch of gravel, his Rolls Royce glided to a halt under the imposing façade of St. James' Keep. The castle's heavy ramparts stared down at the sea from the most remote headland on the Gower Peninsula.

Cathcart was late for his meeting of the Prometheus Group.

Prometheus was a clandestine society of senior Whitehall mandarins, shadow-walkers disaffected by current thinking in the upper echelons of power in London. When the politicians or the judges failed to act, the Prometheus Group was there to intervene and restore the balance.

The Promethians acted within the law where possible, and outside the law where necessary.

Cathcart remembered the myth from his classics studies at Eton. Prometheus – the Greek warrior who rejected the Gods and suffered a terrible, eternal retribution for his treason. Lashed to a rock for all eternity, his liver devoured every day by an avenging eagle. "On a remote, rocky outcrop. Well, we've come to the right place," he thought, glancing to the black cliff and the ocean below, as he ran up the steps from his car.

Cathcart swept order into his wind-tousled hair, and tugged on the bell-pull to the right of the door.

The journey from London had taken three hours. Ample time to reflect on the pink dossier with the eagle motif that he carried under his arm, and on the conversation earlier in the week with Sir Geraint Welles, squire of St. James' and the original Promethian.

Even in the corridors of Whitehall, the existence of Prometheus was an absolute secret. Only eight people knew of its existence. They were its members, six of whom were now sipping sherry in the great dining hall of the Keep.

Cathcart could sense that this meeting was not a minor matter. There would be no talk of marginalising a troublesome civil servant, or arranging for some gangland thugs to threaten a dissident backbencher. In any case, trivial matters such as these would have come under 'normal business' back at the office.

For Prometheus to convene, something far more serious was looming. Something that had already strained the faces in the drawing room, even that of Simone Ellingham, a medium-level functionary in MI6 called into the group as the protegee of Welles. With only six years of membership, Ellingham was still the newest Promethian.

"Let us dine," said Welles, smiling benevolently to his colleagues as he pressed a button on the wall. "We can get down to business once we are refreshed. What is it old Gennadi Zhirinovski from the KGB used to say? *A well-fed worker is a happy worker.*"

*****

"Unthinkable."

Simone Ellingham's voice was trembling. "This utterly, utterly contravenes even the broadest definition of our ethical code."

Geoffrey Chalfont, deputy director of operations at MI6, folded his arms. It had been some time since he had seen Ellingham so distraught.

Sir Geraint Welles stepped into the breach.

"Simone, current thinking inside No.10 bases itself upon the Downing Street Declaration, as you know. In it, her Majesty's government, in its infinite wisdom, countenances the possibility of a united Ireland. Our duty to preserve the integrity of the kingdom includes preserving Northern Ireland as a sovereign territory. We can hardly have fought the Argentinians for a distant outpost, only to consider relinquishing a territory here at home. No matter how you define our allegiance as loyal servants, our duty as private citizens – as 'Promethians' – is clear. We must disable this so-called 'peace process', before it goes too far."

Ellingham was not convinced. "Geraint, the Declaration states on five separate occasions that no such change is possible without majority consent. I cannot see how our sovereignty could be impugned. Besides, the method you are suggesting is pure lunacy. Targeting a royal! If we lay hands on one of our own, then we are as evil as those we seek to defeat."

Chalfont leaned forward in his chair. "Ma'am, Sir Geraint is quite right. This is a complex matter, and quite apart from the integrity of the realm, there are other issues. If this process stays on track, then the terrorist, it would appear, has won. Presumably you would accept that we cannot allow that. Therefore, it becomes an issue we must deal with. It becomes a simple question of strategy. An ordinary target, whether military or civilian, is simply not enough.

"This time, we require more than an atrocity. We require an outrage."

Chalfont paused for a second to let his words sink in. Then he administered the *coup de grace.*

"These are the perpetrators of Warrenpoint, these are the men behind the Mountbatten killing. And only an exceptional public outcry can block their progress."

Chalfont's choice of example was a calculated one. He knew Mountbatten had sought the advice of MI6 before travelling to his death in Ireland. He knew that their response had been that it was an 'acceptable risk'. And he knew the memo had been signed by Simone Ellingham.

Her face remained impassive as he finished, and settled back with his tumbler of brandy.

Welles had his back to the party. He was looking up at a stag's head, mounted on the wall. "Ladies and gentlemen, we have been reduced to defending ourselves like animals. Sometimes, that requires personal suffering. Like a beast that sacrifices a limb to escape from a snare. We are forced to harm one of our own."

He turned to face them. "I fear nothing less will give us the impetus we need."

"I agree wholeheartedly," said Sir Anthony Cathcart. "I was at Ampleforth with Nairac. His killers now wear expensive suits. His former colleagues, meanwhile, are shown the door. I ran into a former operative of ours in Oxford last month. Some of you may even remember Steve Gregson. He's stacking shelves in a supermarket now."

He cast his eyes around the room, and brought them to rest on the dissenter. "But I digress. The territorial issue is the key," Cathcart continued. "It is very simple. We must defend the integrity of the realm. We have no choice."

The other members of Prometheus, seated, brandies in hand, around the fireplace, nodded. Sir Peter Deans was a former barrister and a retired director of MI6. Francis Anderton, a former assistant to Deans, was currently a special advisor on security to her Majesty. Richard Oland, a former brigadier in the Queen's Own Highlanders, was now on secondment from MI6 to the Prime Minister's Office.

They all knew that agreement by five members of Prometheus was sufficient for a proposal to be approved.

The lady, alas, would protest in vain.

*****

Four shots jerked Simone Ellingham out of a fitful sleep.

She swept back the heavy satin curtain of the bedroom in the Keep's east wing, and peered out across the estate. A light mist had drifted in from the sea during the night. Her travel clock told her it was 7.20am.

A figure in a wax jacket half a mile away over the fields had the familiar profile of Sir Geraint. He was holding the shotgun that had fired the shots. The leaner figure beside him was either Anderton or Deans.

She was irritated at his lack of consideration in hunting close to the house at an early hour. But she was more irritated at herself, for having overslept.

In twenty minutes, Ellingham was showered and dressed. She descended the main stairway on to the ornate mosaic marble of the entrance hall.

She cursed the veil of secrecy that prevented the use of an official helicopter. She resolved to be on the road to London by eight. It was Saturday morning, and traffic would be light until noon. She would be in Whitehall for lunch.

Welles and Deans were approaching the house as she stepped through the front door into the frosty air. Welles was carrying his shotgun slung lazily over his right forearm. Two crows, lashed together with string, dangled from his left wrist.

"Simone! I almost called you to join us for a bracing walk! Then I thought better of disturbing you," he lied. "Sleep well? Cook will get you some breakfast."

Deans smiled, and slipped past her into the house. Ellingham could sense that he was distant. She had a distinct feeling that her dissent had placed her outside the group.

"Don't worry Geraint, I think I'll make an early start. It's another working Saturday for me, I'm afraid."

"Ah. As you wish." Welles nodded and took her arm, leading her down the steps. He was regarding her with a look somewhere between sympathy and concern.

"Look Simone, just want to be sure we can count on you in this. I understand your reservations. We all share them, of course. Nothing black and white, far from it. No reason to break rank, though. The group has never been split on anything before. It's a case of desperate measures in a bloody awful situation."

"Do you have a particular royal in mind?" said Ellingham, crisply. "From the second division? One of the cousins, perhaps?"

She regretted her sharpness immediately, and forced a weary smile.

"I'm sorry, Geraint. I shall acquiesce, of course. It is the will of the group."

Welles gave a somewhat tortured look of gratitude.

"What about the contract?" Ellingham said.

Welles looked at the ground. "Oland is handling that. I'm suggesting we take it outside the country. Anderton can access some undeclared IRA weaponry. He'll give us the details at our next meeting."

He looked at Ellingham. No matter what she said, her dilemma was written all over her face. He wanted to change the subject.

"Such a pity, really. That it's come to this. Not just for us, for the Irish. Such nice people. So sad."

Welles realised he was still clutching the pair of dead crows.

"Oh. These blackguards. Always interfering with the maize seedlings in my upper meadow. What was it that nice poet chap wrote? Something about farming. *'On a well-kept farm, pests have to be kept down.'*"

*****

103

James Ellingham had 37 mosquitos covering his forearm, when his daughter opened the door from the cottage and stepped down into the glasshouse.

"God, daddy," she said, "I still shudder when I see you do that. You'll catch a nasty infection from those creatures one day, you know."

"That's hardly likely, my dear. After all, they have fed only on my blood in their short lives. I'm hardly likely to infect myself. Besides, without blood, these ladies cannot make their eggs," he said with a tired smile. He had been expecting her.

"It's all about sex. Sex, and survival. And only the female of the species bites. Remarkable how, wherever we look, nature is full of hidden messages."

Simone Ellingham was long past being goaded by her father. She propped herself on the edge of the same wooden workbench where, forty years ago, she had sat as a girl, her thin legs dangling.

An assortment of large, leafy rubber plants shaded the glass tanks where James Ellingham kept his collection of mosquitos and tropical moths. Piping, thermometers and a humidity meter peered between the broad leaves and, from the back of the building, came the gentle trickle of a small rock pool.

"I've given some thought to what you told me. I have a name for you, but I'm out of touch and you'll have to follow it up yourself. That will be difficult. But the information is in the files. Somewhere."

"Am I breaking ranks, daddy? For once, my famous moralistic certainty has deserted me. I can't see what is the greater good. Or, should I say, the lesser evil."

James Ellingham squinted at the small carpet of black shapes feeding on his blood. This time, the only service he could do his daughter was to have certainty, where she had none. "No, they are going a step too far. Alas, yet again, opportunity has been given to the wrong people."

He raised his red-rimmed and watery eyes, allowed her to dive deep into them and reassure herself.

"The contact's name is Quila. That's a codename, of course. Quila was active in Berlin in the 1970s, when I was there, and can be trusted absolutely. I've not had contact since, though. Quila could be hard to trace, and you will be making tracks if you enquire.

Be careful to cover your trail."

"Checking the archive will be difficult. Even my movements are recorded there, these days," she said.

"You won't need to. I ... er ... I have the relevant files here," he said, raising his eyebrows as if anticipating her surprise.

"Breach of protocol, I know."

"Minor act of treason," said Simone.

"Quite. Others would say: a little insurance. Watching your back. The 70s were a difficult time. Ireland, Gaddafi, and all that. And then '82 and the Falklands. They've drawn, shall we say, a veil of reticence over all that now. But some day, someone may draw the veil back a little. Memoirs, that sort of thing. Quite a few of our people have become disillusioned, especially as the nature of the work precludes public recognition. Let's say that I want to show what my contribution was. Or more to the point – what it wasn't."

"You're distancing yourself from our colleagues in the dirty tricks division?"

James Ellingham paused for half a minute, lost in thought, as if he had not heard. "Dirty tricks is a myth. Created by our detractors, darling, as you well know."

Canny old fox, she thought.

"Now," he said, sliding open the front of the glass cubicle.

"I'll show the ladies back into their room, and we can go inside and have a cup of tea."

*****

Simone Ellingham had broken the code for the second time in a week.

In the top floor of her Belsize Park apartment, she slotted her father's CD into her computer, and surveyed the leafy park below. Bringing home an official document was *infra dig* for an MI6 operative, even the unit head. Bringing home an entire section of the official archive would have her sent to the Tower.

As the files loaded, she took a brandy globe from the Hepplewhite cabinet, and poured herself a generous measure of Remy Martin. She had been doing that more often of late.

She lit up a More cigarillo, watching the reflection of the matchlight in the computer screen before her.

"Thirty-six years of service," she thought, recalling how her father had been in the Department for as long as she could remember. "...reduced to a single little silver disc."

The first search for 'Quila' drew a blank. This did not surprise her. Most contacts had a second codename for use in internal files. She would ring her father and ask him. But it was 11.40pm, he would be in bed. Time for some lateral thinking.

She closed down her father's records, switched to the internet, and did a general search for 'Quila'. She scanned the 13 results for anything relating to Berlin or Eastern Germany.

One result leaped off the page at her. Had she not known her father and his taste for the peculiar and grotesque, she would have disregarded it. As it was, it stuck in her like a hook.

"Greenland: the Quilakitsok Mummies. Exhibition. Imperial Museum, Copenhagen, July-September 1972."

She switched back into her father's files and in the folder 'Scandinavia/Arctic'her search produced two references for Greenland. One was a contact named Rovsen, a renegade from Quaanuk who provided information on suspected infiltration of a Greenland oil rig by Greenpeace activists in 1982.

The second name was Eddie, confirmed in the notes as recruited by James Ellingham in Copenhagen in 1972. "Jackpot," she muttered, squeezing the cigarillo between her lips.

In his personal notes she confirmed the external codename: 'Eddie'.

"Hope you enjoyed the mummies, daddy," she whispered into the glass globe, before taking another sip of Remy.

*****

Standing on the threshold of Simone Ellingham's office, a polycup of coffee in either hand, Sir Anthony Cathcart bore a passing resemblance to the statue of Justice a mile away at the Old Bailey.

"She's not here," he said, baffled.

"Miss Ellingham is working from home this morning," said Jeannine, Ellingham's slightly stuffy girl Friday, in a tone that showed her annoyance at being bypassed – even by a Sir.

At that moment, on a leafy residential street in Pimlico, Simone Ellingham padded to a halt before an impressive white façade with an ornate brass 76 on the pillar by the door. She was wearing a royal blue tracksuit and white sneakers. A mauve sweatband, dark with fresh perspiration, clung to her forehead. She held the iron railings while she caught her breath, and looked back along the route of her two-mile jog.

"Gracious. A woman of mettle!" The cheery face of Pamela Dickinson peered round the black door as she pulled it open. "And just in time for a coffee!" She bustled away into the shadows, leaving the door ajar as the jogger wearily climbed the steps.

Ellingham raised the beaker of milky coffee to her lips and felt the warmth flow over her cheeks. Her nose was ruddy from the cold.

She had only once before asked to make a phone call from Pamela's. Her friend was curious. "Anything you can talk about?" she said, replacing the coffee globe on the hotplate. In her left hand, she was squeezing a rubber exerciser shaped like a bright red apple.

Dickinson had trained with Ellingham as a field operative, but had to take an early pension when she got too close to a mortar shell on the Chechnyan border. Nowadays, she mockingly called herself a piece of 'human engineering', due to the number of pins in her femur and upper arm.

Ellingham put down her coffee mug. "Oh, nothing too hush-hush. Just a few non-routine enquiries, really. Trying to trace an old contact of dad's. I didn't want to ring from the office."

She opened her fleece and pulled a brown manila envelope out of the waistband of her sweatpants. "Shouldn't take too long."

"I'll wait for you in the lounge."

As Dickinson closed the door, Ellingham dialled the number listed for Eddie in her father's file. It was an Irish listing she had identified by the code as Maynooth, a commuter town to Dublin and home to one of Ireland's leading universities and seminaries. *Is Eddie a German-speaking Irish theologian?* she thought. Nothing would surprise her.

The phone clicked at the other end. A woman's voice. Ellingham still had only the codenames. This could be a tricky conversation.

She decided to gamble. If she went for the common name first, at least she could pretend it was a wrong number.

"May I speak to Eddie?"

Silence. A long, long silence that grew more deafening until every flicker on the line crackled like an electric shock.

"Eddie has a new address. Langley Cottage, Hepton Rise."

Simone Ellingham froze. Her knuckles whitened round the telephone handset. She turned, knocked her coffee on to the floor, and cursed inwardly.

It was her father's home address.

There was only one possible solution.

"I'm keen to contact Eddie. Or Quila."

Another long pause. Ellingham felt blood pounding in the sides of her neck, with the force of a river in whitewater rapids.

"I haven't been called by that name in almost 20 years," the woman said. "You must be Simone. James told me you might call."

Utter, utter relief. "Yes. I'm rather keen to speak to you."

Simone Ellingham smiled. Even at 48, she still took pleasure in her father's little tests.

*****

DUBLIN, FOUR DAYS LATER

Stephen Maxwell's rainbow scarf billowed in his wake, as he scurried across the Halfpenny Bridge and along Ormond Quay to the Winding Stair Bookshop Café.

A tousle-haired youth grunted 'Morning' to him as he passed. He recognised him as one of his students, from his comparative linguistics course at the university. Under normal circumstances, he might have stopped for a chat. Today, however, he was more hurried than on a normal day on the college cobblestones. Today, he was on a mission for the state.

Maxwell was a little late. Evelyn de Burca was seated by the window on the third floor, reading her *Irish Times* in front of a steaming cappucino. As usual, she had moved herself into the modern history section. It was where she felt most at ease.

He flustered his way between the bookshelves with his coffee. He squeezed past a group of English tourists chatting gaily in the corner about their plans for the day, and laid his manila folders in a disordered heap on the table. An orange flier proclaming opposition to American foreign policy fluttered to the floor. Maxwell let the issue lie.

"Hello, Evelyn, sorry for the delay. The 'academic ten minutes'. Car is in the garage, so it was Shank's Mare this morning, I'm afraid." His voice had an unaccustomed zest. These occasional involvements in the mysterious workings of Foreign Affairs gave him a vicarious thrill.

Evelyn would not mind. Even as undergraduates, when they had worked on the college newspaper together, he had never made a deadline.

He rummaged through his papers. "Just begun working with different colours – speeds up file management. Yellow for lectures, the blue for notes, pink and orange for extra-curricular. Here we are," he muttered. He grinned as he tugged two sheets of pink paper, held together by a staple, from the middle of the bundle.

He glanced over her shoulder to ensure that the tourists were not listening. They were far away, engrossed in discussions about Celtic burial grounds in Meath.

"So. First of all, that 's your tape back again. Yes. Well, your friend Simone wasn't too hard to pin down. She doesn't seem to have moved around too much."

Maxwell was beginning his performance. He was relishing the chance to display his skill on his home ground. "I've done the full dialect analysis. She's about 50. Never been away from the UK, not for any length of time. Childhood in the west midlands, Nottingham or Lincolnshire. After that, early teens on the south coast. Probably a quality boarding school – some conscious effort made to eradicate the home accent. And only public schoolgirls say 'keen' any more – although mostly in relation to boys. Anyway, after that, several years in Oxfordshire. Since she's educated, probably the university. More recently, London. The sparseness and low frequency of adjectives usually indicates an administrative environment," he said.

"Put that all together, and my guess is a career woman. In either government, Scotland Yard, or Whitehall."

Maxwell read de Burca's face. He could see that he was on target. His chest swelled as he swooped into the final act. "Oh, and she's not in her office. It's tiled. A kitchen, or a bathroom maybe. She's also in private – it's a landline, not a mobile. And the radio in the background would also indicate that she's at home. Sandy Posey, *The Single Girl.* Mid-sixties. I'd say our lady listens to BBC Radio 2."

On the phone, De Burca had not noticed the background music behind Ellingham's voice.

"Thanks. Just wanted to double-check she was who she said she was," said de Burca. "Now I'm sure."

Triumphant, Maxwell passed her the pink sheet with his bullet points.

"Stephen, you never fail to amaze me. Hope it didn't take you too long."

The mere suggestion was a challenge. Maxwell sharpened his ears. It was time for an impromptu encore.

"The three English girls behind you. Let's start with Miss Ponytail. From Devon originally, grew up close to, but not in, London. I'd say she works in recruitment or training – she's said 'use your initiative' twice in twenty minutes. Then there's Miss Spectacles – she's a thoroughbred Londoner. Probably Stoke Newington or Golders Green. Occasional Jewish inflections – but it's not her own background. The third one, though, is the interesting one. Norfolk originally, but she has a particular sociolect that can mean only one thing."

He lowered his voice to a whisper. "She's done time. Several years at least. And probably in Strangeways."

He paused, basking in the glow of de Burca's admiration.

"You see, Evelyn? You just never know who you're dealing with."

11

BELFAST, AUTUMN 2004

"Montblanc. Nice pen," Tom Black thought to himself, looking at the loose-leaf folder of notes on the desk to his left.

The Strellsen jacket slung over the chair beside him belonged to Jimmy Williamson, head of the Unionist People's Group and a founder member of Black's think-tank on the fringes of the peace negotiations.

The group was his first initiative in his new role as mediator – a sounding board for proposals on the process, as they emerged from Dublin and from London.

The meeting was over. Williamson picked up his jacket and turned to Black. "Tom, you talk a lot of sense for a military man."

"No less than yourself, Jimmy," said Black, scrutinising Williamson's face for a reaction.

Williamson smiled at the veiled joke. He had never publicly admitted to membership of the paramilitary wing, despite spending seven years in Long Kesh prison. Under other circumstances, the barman he had gunned down in Twinbrook in 1971 might have been at the same negotiating table.

Outside, a grey rain cascaded down the serried steps of Stormont Castle. The vast complex sat like a forlorn slab of white stone in the waterlogged landscape.

Twenty minutes later, Black's jeep swept out from the castle grounds on to the shiny tarmac of the Dublin road. The drive to Ardsallagh would take three hours, the last of them would be in darkness.

Williamson and his assistant Robbie Pearson would spend a day as Black's guests, returning to Belfast on Sunday. Black saw it as a 'getting to know you' exercise.

Pearson sat behind, sullen and withdrawn, almost invisible in the shadows. Due to his swarthy skin, they called him 'Chocca' in loyalist circles.

Black sensed that he could work with Williamson.

Williamson in turn saw Black as a necessary evil: a workable Catholic, part of the new order.

Chocca Pearson, on the other hand, would have been happy to choke him with a fish-wire.

*****

The package had been left on the sideboard by Mary Gallagher, the new housekeeper from the village. She seemed particular and efficient, but had a disconcerting habit of leaving doors open wherever she went in the house.

"It helps the air circulate," she had said, when Tom Black mentioned it. Mary was a woman of few words. It was a quality, he decided, he would come to appreciate.

He opened the envelope while Jimmy Williamson and Chocca Pearson were upstairs, no doubt noticing his unpainted bedrooms through Mary's open doors.

He replaced the contents of the package, and locked it in his desk.

*****

'Jerky' Gopalan was chopping a chicken and cursing a Taoiseach. Downing Street had vetoed the Jamaican menu he had planned for the visit of the Prime Minister of Ireland.

Based on latest intelligence from Dublin, James Foley's favourite dish was, according to Number 10, now 'Balti Chicken – Delhi Style'. The Prime Minister's public relations people had sent the order ten minutes before, with apologies for the short notice. The meal was due on the table in two hours.

Jerky's parents were from Spanish Town, Jamaica, but he was a London boy. Closest he had been to an Indian was playing Tonto with his schoolmates, on the streets of Ealing in the 60s.

His Lone Ranger had been Joe Swarbriggs, now his sous-chef in the kitchen of The Mango House, the chic restaurant he ran in London's Soho. In the Mango House kitchens, the atmosphere was frantic.

"Fuck Foley," said Joe, pulping galangal under a broad-blade knife with a little more elbow than usual. "How are we supposed to know how they do it in fucking Delhi?"

Jerky grinned at him through the steel shelves.

"He'll just have to settle for London-Delhi."

*****

De Vries had flown into Carrickfin, but Black had been preoccupied with his guests, and could not meet him there. Williamson and Pearson had been collected two hours before by an official driver, and were on their way back to Belfast.

Black had taken them round the Inishowen 100 Scenic Drive the previous day. Chocca had declined to stroll on Five Finger Strand when Black had told him it was the site of a famous IRA arms find some years ago. On the whole, however, the buddy-buddy exercise had been a success.

Jacques De Vries clambered out of the taxi that halted at the front entrance of Ardsallagh, weary from the journey, but reinvigorated by the journey's end. He wanted a seat by the fire, heat in his bones, and one of the hot whiskeys now famous on La Réunion as a 'Tom Black'.

They went into the lounge. There was something Black needed to discuss. He did not offer a bed. Not yet. De Vries could sleep later.

From the desk, Black produced the crumpled brown envelope that had been waiting for him on his return from Stormont. He unwrapped the contents, and placed them on the tabletop.

"It had a Brussels postmark. A photocopy. An article from *La Provence*. It's nearly a year old."

De Vries took the photocopy and read the headline. "I remember this paper from my Legion induction in Marseilles."

"The article deals with the assassination of King Alexander of Czechoslovakia there on October 9th, 1934," said Black.

"The French Foreign Minister, Louis Barthou, died with him. They were in a vehicle cavalcade driving through the town. The assassin's name was Veliko Kerin. He was sent by the Croatian

113

Ustachis, who hated Alexander because he was a Serb. Kerin was a press photographer, and got close enough to jump up on the running-board of the limo. He managed to put a bullet in the King's chest, before being cut down by a guard with a sabre," said Black.

"And was then also lynched by the crowd," said de Vries.

"Right," said Black. "At the same time, Barthou was wounded, and bled to death in the confusion."

"1934 is hardly the other day," said de Vries, "What has this got to do with you?"

"It arrived in yesterday's post. It must be linked to my work here as a mediator. After that, there could be several possibilities. The most obvious is a warning. A hit on a public figure? A politician, a royal, maybe even a Prime Minister or a Taoiseach. I'm looking forward to telling Foley," said Black.

"Aren't there threats like that every week over here?" said de Vries.

"Sure. But it's higher-risk at the moment. We're at a crucial stage in the peace talks. The crazies from the IRA and the UVF out there know they won't get a slice of the new order. They would do anything to disrupt the negotiations," said Black.

De Vries was feeling uncomfortable. In Irish affairs, he was out of his depth. "So what will you do?"

"I'll check out Jimmy Williamson. Maybe he's heard something from the loyalist side. And O'Hagan will sound out the Republicans for me. First, though, we've to do some digging of our own. I'm beginning to realise why Foley wanted someone floating between the parties. He's more of a politician than he lets on."

Black reached out, and took the article back.

"But there's something more. We aren't finished with our unlucky friends in Marseilles quite yet," he said.

"It didn't come out until years later. There was a cover-up. It appears that Kerin only managed to wound the King. The lethal bullet was a shot to the heart – but it entered him from behind."

For the second time in a morning, De Vries was feeling like a dunce. "A second gunman?"

"Jacques, we both know the National Guard are ... impossible to underestimate. It was a bullet from his own minders. They were returning fire, but they killed him on the spot.

"And as for Barthou, it turned out that his wound wasn't from the assassin, either. His bullet was standard issue – from the pistol carried by the French police."

"So both of them were killed..."

"...by their own people," Black finished de V's sentence.

"That means that this hit, if there is one, will be an inside job," said de V.

"The context in which it happened is interesting too," said Black.

"King Alexander was attempting to forge a new alliance with the French. Perhaps the Croats saw this as a strengthening of his Serbian faction in their home country, which would have been a threat to them. Not unlike the position here for Unionists fearful of Republicans."

"So the Croats tried to take out the man at the centre of the alliance," said de Vries, struggling. It was a hot whiskey he had wanted, not a lesson in French history.

"No, they did not want to kill the individual. It was what he represented. They weren't assassinating a person, they were assassinating the whole political process," said Black.

Understanding had dawned on de Vries. "A brazen attempt to change the course of history."

He sighed, and brushed back his hair with his fingers. The small-pond politics of La Réunion seemed petty, and so very far away.

*****

At that moment in No. 10, Downing Street, Foley was taking morning coffee with Harold Fowlds, the Prime Minister's personal advisor on Northern Ireland. The topic of discussion was Tom Black.

"It all seems to be going rather swimmingly," said Fowlds.

Coming from a comprehensive school in Yorkshire, Fowlds thought his plain English needed tarting up with a smattering of phrases from P.G. Wodehouse.

"He's too much of a patchwork to be a hate figure. He's charming, charismatic, self-made millionaire, a rather clever manipulator, an ex-soldier, and a Francophile. The Irish paramilitaries respect the legionnaire; the politicians respect the businessman; and he has us all feeling just a tad guilty for so disliking the French."

Foley laughed heartily before responding. He knew exactly how Fowlds needed to be stroked. "I'm surprised to hear an upper-crust

Englishman say anything negative about the French," he said.

"But you're right," Foley went on. "Tom Black is exactly what we need. A neutral channel for free flow of communication, with no prejudice. He even had Jimmy Williamson walking the beaches of Donegal at the weekend. I'm surprised the sand didn't burn his feet."

At the back of the house, a yellow van drew up. The two men who alighted, dressed in identical overalls, were stressed and tense.

The sign on the van read 'The Mango House. Caribbean Cuisine. Jamaican dishes a speciality."

*****

De Vries had cast politeness aside, and asked for a whiskey outright. Black poured the steaming water into the two glasses. De V accepted his gratefully.

"Remember Stiefelmann, that crazy Swiss who went back to Africa again after the Legion? I heard he got hired to go after Amin, but he screwed up and got caught at the border," said de Vries.

"I was surprised he got that far," said Black, counting four cloves to each glass. "The guy was a fool."

"Well, he got away from the Ugandan police, but not from his client," said de Vries. "That was his big mistake, thinking he was safe once he made it out of Uganda and over to Kenya. But Stiefelmann knew who was behind the plot, so he had to be silenced. They found him a month later in a back alley in Nairobi. Died of low blood pressure. On account of having his throat cut."

Black smiled at de V's rather black humour.

"Tom, what I'm saying is, if you are being tipped off about a hit, it can't go outside this room. Otherwise, the next target could be you. Was there anything else in the package?"

"A bar of chocolate. Belgian chocolate. Neuhaus," said Black, handing it over.

De Vries turned the tablet of chocolate over in his hands. It was time to redeem himself with some sharp analysis.

"You said it came from Brussels. But the barcode is covered by a label printed in English. Could have been bought here. Or in the UK. And the photocopy of the article is on watermarked paper. *La Corsaire*. That's the brand of the French civil service. Presumably also for their offices in the European Parliament. Maybe an official of *l'administration* in Brussels."

Black smiled, and lifted the phone. "Only a very few people know my preference in chocolate. People, for instance, who've received chocolates from me. People I've had to apologise to."

He looked out the French window to the Donegal hills. It was 3.30pm in Ardsallagh. It was 4.30pm in Brussels.

He punched 14 digits into the black handset, and stared at the sky, as if willing the signal on its way. As the connection was made, he lowered his eyes.

"Thank you for the chocolate, Evelyn."

*****

Black replenished the glasses with another couple of hot whiskeys, and added coal to the fire.

He had filled de Vries in on who Evelyn de Burca was.

"Do you trust her?" said de Vries.

"Absolutely. We go back years. I didn't – wouldn't – ask her for her source. Evelyn is no fool. If she's taking this seriously, there's a contract out there. On a senior politician, or one of the other key players. If she's passed it to me, I'd guess she regards it as international."

He paused for thought, sipping distractedly from the steaming whiskey.

De Vries tore back the wrapper, and snapped off the corner of the chocolate. His analysis leading to a French civil servant had been somewhat wide of the mark. There was irritation in his voice again.

"If the chocolate was a private clue, then why bother coding the message? Why this newspaper article? She could simply have called you."

"To avoid interception, I suppose. Without knowing the significance of Neuhaus, the message has no source. Although, knowing Evelyn, I'd say it was just as likely pure mischief."

"So what do we do next?" asked de Vries, grimacing at the intermingling flavours of whiskey and cocoa.

"We can't follow this up by phone. Old debts have to be called in personally. The jet's over at Carrickfin.

"We're going to talk to Domino."

*****

Black cursed as his head knocked the lintel of the workshop door. The hollow tinkle of a small bell announced his arrival.

In the dock outside, a cargo ship with building products from southern China was filling the air with lime-dust, as the forty-footers rolled along the quay. The sun was an orange ball on the horizon, and dusk was rolling in.

De Vries did not know Domino, and had stayed back at the hotel.

There was no-one in sight. As Black's eyes adjusted to the dimness, shapes emerged from the gloom at the back of the long room.

In the window he could see the New York skyline, glittering lights and the pinnacle of the Empire State Building punching upward from the ragged silhouette of Manhattan. The room was filled with the pungent aroma of linseed oil, cheap varnish and balsa sawdust. The wall was filled with half-used paintpots of all colours.

A door creaked open to the right, and a tall shadow stepped in. His hands were broad as the power shovels rattling outside on the docks. His denim dungarees were mottled with a rainbow of colours.

"Welcome to Marseilles, mon vieux!" he exclaimed, "you haven't changed a bit."

He came up to Black, and the two men embraced. "What's it to be? Coffee or cognac?"

"How is the cognac?" said Black, smiling.

"Only the best. And the coffee is shit," beamed Domino, taking two shot glasses from the shelf, and a bottle from behind the paintpots.

Black pointed to the model skyline. "So this is what you do. Impressive. I almost believed I was in New York."

"That's for some damn book-keeper. The poor *imbécile* thinks having Manhattan on the wall of his apartment will help him get women. Somebody should break it to him: it doesn't happen to an accountant. *Salud!*"

Black savoured the brandy burning the dust of the docks from his throat. Domino refilled the glasses, and propped himself on the edge of his work-table. He downed his glass in one and turned it upside-down on the rough wood.

"Mostly I do sets for the theatre, and for the television people. God, I've been at it for fifteen years now. I have a small group of loyal customers, they keep me busy. Even Chabrol has looked in. You remember that one with Romy Schneider? I did the police investigation room," he said.

Black nodded solemnly. He had not seen the film.

"Now and again there is also specialist work for the ad agencies. Dull as hell, and they're a bunch of *salauds*, but they pay well."

He plucked a colour printout from the notice board. "My latest masterpiece."

The face of a grinning actor beamed out from a tapered frame that represented an angel cake. "It took seventeen hours to build. The icing is pure gelatine," said Domino, with obvious pride. Black nodded. He pinned the photo back on to the wall.

"We have to talk," said Domino. He slid the door sign to 'Closed' and pulled on his jacket. "Let's take a walk," he said.

They stepped up into the street and proceeded down towards the Vieux Port, carefully picking their way through the poverty of the Le Panier district, and across the Place des Moulins. Black could just hear Domino's voice above the clamour of goods vehicles, and the piercing whistles of fork-lifts reversing.

Laden trucks were streaming up from the waterfront, like worker ants returning to their nest. It was the noise of money being made.

Domino lit up a rolled cigarette. "Colombian. It's the only thing that keeps me going in this shit-hole," he said. In his heavy, yellowed fingers, the fat joint looked spindly as a matchstick.

From the pocket of his black serge jacket, Domino produced a patent leather hip flask with an oak leaf motif. "More brandy, *mon vieux*. It will keep this cold out of your bones."

Black took a swig from the flask.

"After you rang me yesterday, I put in a call to Schaffer at *La Deuxième*. As usual, he's nervous as hell. No word back as yet, but he'll be in touch. I'll wait until tonight, and ring him again. If something has come down through the network, he will be the first in Marseilles to know. Of course, if it's a private deal, he might not. Until the trigger is pulled."

Black shared Domino's faith in *La Deuxième*. It was the public face of the Legion, the communications office that fielded all contact between the regiment and the general population, even the families of the legionnaires. Schaffer was a hunched little captain with a lucrative sideline linking up ex-legionnaires with anyone looking for a soldier with a gun.

If word was out about a contract in London or Belfast, Schaffer would be there like a weasel, greedy-eyed and eager to set up a connection.

For his customary five per cent up front, of course.

And what Schaffer knew, Domino would know by midnight.

*****

At 11.27pm, Black and De Vries were on their third bottle of Nuit St. Georges at La Mer Rouge. Black usually preferred the Hilton, but he wanted to keep out of sight on this visit.

Below the hotel window, only the occasional taxi and the night bus broke the silence.

When it came, the ringing of the phone was unusually loud, and both men started.

"Dominique," said Black, and settled back to listen. De Vries tried to read his face. The wine had dulled their senses. All he could see was the exhaustion in Black's eyes. After ten minutes, Black muttered 'Merci' and replaced the receiver.

"Jesus," he said. "Somebody has put out a contract on a cousin of the Prince."

12

MARSEILLES

Shaffer chainsmoked when he was nervous.

He was chainsmoking now. Four cigarette ends lay flattened in the oily puddle at his feet, as Domino's bulky silhouette lurched down the concrete slope into the underground car park.

Shaffer's weasel face carried a small scar on the right cheek. It was a souvenir of a duel with sabres, his initiation ceremony into the student fraternity at the University of Heidelberg. That was before he came to the Legion. He was one of the few with an education, and it had landed him the comfortable desk job in 'la Deuxième'.

Marseilles was in a cold snap, and Domino could see his breath in the air. "*Merde!*" he gasped, causing Shaffer to startle and spin to face him. The orange tip of his cigarette floated like a firefly in the darkness.

"Look Shaffer, we can't talk here. This undercover shit is like something out of Georges Simenon. I'm freezing. I know a bar where we can go. Don't worry, nobody will know you there. It's too fucking respectable." Domino did not wait for a reply. He strode off towards the lift.

Shaffer didn't argue. Domino had kept him standing for twenty minutes, and he badly needed to visit the rest room.

They found a booth at the back of *La Sauterelle* on the Rue des Pauvres. A candle in the centre of the table lit up the two faces like a cheap reproduction Dutch painting. One of the cloth roses in the vase bore the dark ring of a cigarette burn.

The waitress brought a silver ashtray and a bottle of pastis.

Shaffer returned from the bathroom, muttering that he would

prefer an espresso. Domino ignored him and slid a small, brimming tumbler across the table. Much as he liked pastis, there was another reason. It would make their chat more interesting.

"Drink it, *mon ami*. You're already nervous enough. An espresso now, and you'd fucking keel over," said Domino. He sighed as the first pastis rolled into his gut like a fireball.

"Why couldn't we do this on the phone? You know I don't like talking about these things on the street. Or in bars either, for that matter," said Shaffer, with a sullen face.

"You know, you always did over-estimate how much attention people pay to you," said Domino.

"Look around. Nobody in this place gives a damn who we are, or what we're doing. There's every language in the world along that bar, they're all off the fucking boats. Besides, I don't want to talk to you over the phone, I want to look into your beady eyes and make sure you're being straight with me."

Shaffer's eyes were still clear. Domino poured more pastis. The second bottle would loosen Shaffer up. Domino, meanwhile, would keep a clear head. There were advantages to being six foot three.

Two women came over from the bar. They had the same red fingernails, but the blonde's white skin made the red seem brighter than on the African woman behind her. The blonde carried an empty tumbler and a cigarette; the African had a half dozen coloured bangles on her wrist. The blonde wore a blue lamé dress, split at the side. The black woman's pink plastic mini-skirt was stretched to bursting point.

The blonde turned to Shaffer. They always go for the little guy first. "Good evening. You know, if you like, we can give you our very personal guided tour of Marseilles."

"No. Thank you," said Shaffer, darting Domino a dark look, as if they had been rumbled already.

She lifted her foot and propped it on the edge of Shaffer's chair. She was wearing no underwear. She was shaved in the shape of a heart. "The answer is still no." He sniggered like a schoolboy and buried his gaze in his fifth pastis.

The blonde frowned and looked around the bar. She moved mechanically away, followed by the African who, Domino suspected, was Sudanese and had no French. The blonde was probably her companion and her pimp at the same time.

When the women were gone, he could see that Shaffer was ready to talk. "So. What about von Scharn?"

Shaffer was gradually feeling more reassured. Domino poured drink number six to help him along.

"Von Scharn still hangs around in Marseilles, he still has a few friends here. He uses *Chez Miriam* behind the Place des Moulins, same whorehouse he's been going to since the 70s. Old habits die hard. He even married a Marseilles girl once, but it didn't last."

"After ten years in the Legion, marriage rarely does," said Domino, ruefully. He had his own tale to tell there.

"Von Scharn drinks with the American, McCreedy, and McCreedy is one of my ... special friends," said Schaffer.

McCreedy was part of the invisible network of information-gatherers Schaffer had built up by bartering the rich flow of tidbits that crossed his desk at 'la Deuxième'.

"Von Scharn turned up at Miriam's last month with a Russian called Paliakov, who is a banker with Moscow Development Bank. Paliakov was at the Hotel Rose, but they had checked in under the name of the woman with him, Nina Trubarova."

"I don't mean to sound like a fucking lawyer," said Domino, "but where are you going with this? We're in Marseilles. The town is coming down with lonely Russians."

"Trubarova was supposed to be his wife. But he still went to the whorehouse. Call me old-fashioned, but that's either unusual, or a bit fucked-up. So I checked it out, and found that Paliakov worked for Moscow Development Bank in London back in the Gorbachov days. They say he was KGB, which is no surprise because there were probably more KGB in that bank than there were British bugs," said Shaffer.

Domino nodded, opening his green cigarette tin. He picked out a clump of tobacco, laid it carefully along the paper, and pared shavings from his block of dope on top.

Shaffer's guard had come down, and he was relishing the tale.

"So a couple of days later, I told McCreedy to find out if there was a job going down. He said Paliakov had told von Scharn that something needed taken care of in England. A termination contract on a 'high security target that had high security protection'. Very dangerous. Possibly the contractor would not get out alive."

"Why von Scharn? Apart from the fact that nobody would miss

that prick," said Domino.

"Von Scharn killed some guy last year in Colombia. It was unusual, a grudge killing for some millionaire car dealer from Texas. Specialist imports and sports prototypes, expensive shit like that. The Colombian was a croupier in a casino in Seattle, ripped the Texan off at the gaming table. When the Texan realised he'd been cheated he took it personally, but by that time the Colombian was back home buying drinks for his compadres in Medellin. To cut a long story short, the Texan hired Von Scharn to go down there and take him out."

"So are we going to see von Scharn feeding the pigeons in Trafalgar Square?" said Domino, grinning. His plan to stay sober had collapsed.

"No. He turned it down. Told McCreedy that security over there's too tight these days, what with bin Laden and the IRA. Said he wouldn't enjoy his earnings cooped up in an English jail. Never mind thirty years of their god-awful fish and chips," sniggered Shaffer.

"And in London, it's not as easy to bribe yourself out of trouble as it is in Colombia."

"Did they tell von Scharn who the mark was?"

"I doubt it. Not before he accepted the job."

"So how did you come up with this 'cousin of the Prince' thing?" said Domino, pointing an accusing finger around his shot glass.

"Relax, Dominique. My sources are ... impeccable," said Shaffer. He was slurring now.

Suddenly, he burst into laughter.

"Just tell Black I rang up the fucking Queen."

*****

De Vries propped his permacup of coffee back on the dashboard, and tried to see through the driving rain.

A sign told him he was 45 kilometres from Dublin. He steered the land cruiser around the sharp bend on to the steep hill that runs from the town of Slane down to the River Boyne.

"What was that thing of yours about the Irish weather, Tom? Ah yes. *You know when it's summer, because the rain gets warmer,*" he said, with a rueful smile.

In the passenger seat, Black was not listening. He snapped his mobile phone shut, and looked across the grounds of Slane Castle on the right.

"Sorry, Jacques. That was a message from Domino. This thing seems to be checking out. He said von Sharn wouldn't touch it , and even that low-life Shaffer has the shits. I can't keep this under wraps any longer. I'll have to tell Foley, when I see him tonight. And before you tell me, I know Foley can't keep this from London. I could be setting myself up."

*****

Just before dawn in Donegal, the sight of four dead crows spiked on an old gate had knocked Tom Black off his stride.

A home-made oak sign bore the gaelic word 'Tearmann' – 'sanctuary' – in faded butter-yellow letters, and around the neck of one of the birds hung the tatters of a red ribbon. Red, to ward off the evil eye from the occupants within.

Black was taking his usual early morning walk in the woods along the margins of Ardsallagh. He had met Foley for an hour the previous night, and then driven back to Donegal.

De Vries, still weary from the drive, was asleep at the house.

Black continued through Cratlagh Wood, a little the colder for passing a place of death.

A hundred yards later, he glanced back at the crows, with an uncomfortable feeling that he was not alone. In the pre-dawn darkness he glimpsed a black shadow, head bowed, moving among the trees at the last bend.

From the trees, he heard the eerie wind-whistle the locals claimed was a harbinger of death, calling for a soul from the cottages in the wood. It was heard at the time of 'day-clearing', as the older ones called the dawn.

Black looked back again. *Keep it inside this room,* de V had said, *otherwise you're a target too.*

Although he was older now, his eyes were still sharp. The forest hung like a theatre set, receding into a darkness so thick the trees melted into black.

The forest seemed to be floating towards him, threatening to envelop and smother him. Nature, Black thought, takes on a menacing form, when coupled with the terrors in our head.

Black peered backwards again, this time for a full minute and a half. Now, no shadows were shifting among the trees, except the occasional leaf trembling in the light breeze.

He began to relax. No follower was there. He was glad to doubt himself.

In Cratlagh Wood the forest floor never dries. It is a constant place of rotting and decay. As Black lifted his feet, his boots sucked the soft mulch. Every step pressed the fallen leaves further into the muddy broth covering the path.

A raven, soaring into the wood from the road below, passed over him and, cawing, sailed up into the tenebrous cathedral of green behind.

Black breathed a sigh of relief as he emerged into the grey light of the morning, now breaking over the road.

*****

Sir Geraint Welles was having a good Friday.

There was a spring in his step as he breezed through the door of the 15 Club at precisely 5.28pm, to round off his day with a tumbler of scotch in the Gentleman's Lounge.

"Good evening, Sir Geraint. How are we today?"

"Excellent Margaret, and all the better for seeing you," effused Welles, handing his beige woollen overcoat to the young hostess who greeted him at the door.

"So you're not going up home for a bit of shooting this weekend?" she asked, turning up her Scottish accent just a fraction and unleashing her best Glaswegian smile. She always rolled her r's a little for Welles. Reminding him of home resulted in a generous tip, especially when he had made a good dent in a bottle of Laphroaig.

Cathcart was already waiting by the fire. Without a word, he took a large cigar with an unusual taper from his waistcoat, and handed it to Welles.

"Davidoff. 'Series Special', Geraint, best I could find. I must concede, you win again."

"Any Davidoff is sweet, Anthony, but one from your good self is the sweetest of all," said Welles. Nothing pleased him more than trumping Cathcart in a bet.

"It was exactly as you predicted, Geraint. Ellingham sent the information to the Irish, and sure enough, it has now come back via Dublin to London. Deans picked it up in the PM's office. He telephoned me this morning.

"Which all presents us with rather a problem, don't you think? Scotland Yard is now on alert, so we have lost the element of surprise. That is to put it mildly. Perhaps we should place the whole operation on hold."

"Oh nonsense, Anthony," said Welles, shifting his rump towards the glowing coals. He caught sight of himself in the gilded Chinese mirror opposite, loosened his tie and undid his collar button.

"As you know, we have the weapon. It will look like an IRA operation. In fact, we're even better off than before. Our loyalist friends, when they learn of our efforts, will be only too happy to assist with our bonus prize."

"And what would that be?" said Cathcart, in the pompous tone he used when he was at a complete loss.

"To remove this rather troublesome 'fixer' of Foley's," said Welles.

He smacked his lips and looked admiringly at three hundred years of his Scottish heritage, swirling in the glass he held in his hand.

"To eliminate the illustrious Mister Black."

*****

It was a cool Saturday. Tom Black hoisted on his waterproof jacket for his second walk of the week.

This time, in the light of afternoon, Cratlagh Wood was a place dappled with sunlight, cascading through the leafy canopy overhead.

Superstitions. Black thought of the gifts at the crossroads on La Réunion. In Donegal, the older folk would still leave out a parcel of buttered wheaten bread, to appease the fairies of the wood.

Superstition and charms were all very well, but Black preferred more practical measures. From a faded chamois pouch he took a six-inch hunting knife, a relic of Africa that he had not held in his hand in sixteen years. He had last used it to slaughter a rabid lemur that threatened to infect the pack on the Madagascar lands.

This morning, a nagging feeling in the back of his neck had told him to take it along.

Probably just imagination, Black told himself, as he left the house by the back door.

The soft mist flowing up the bay to Cratlagh sprinkled a cast of silver over his shoulders and tweed cap. The sound of the wind from the bay petered into silence as he entered the back end of the wood, leaving only the sound of his footsteps. The crows' nests, high and deep in the branches, foretold storm weather ahead.

At the next corner he would again pass the gate of Tearmann, gaze into the hollow eye sockets of the blinded crows.

Death's indifferent gaze was causing Black to reflect. He knew that all he had done in his life was ephemeral. It would disappear, while only the wind and the fresh rain would remain.

With no children he would be, as they said in Donegal, 'the last of the name'. The thought saddened him.

Passing Tearmann, he followed the track to the left, and gently descended through the heart of the wood.

He first became aware of the follower when a clutch of sparrows, rattled by the snap of a twig a hundred yards behind him, flew out like a dozen scraps of cinder tumbling in the air.

Black's hunting instincts were still strong. Ahead, he would need an extra hundred yards' lead over the follower, in order to break line of sight on the twisting path. There was no chance of gaining that lead.

Pressing the knife to his hip, he lunged to the right, into the thicket that skirted the path. He pushed forward thirty yards, then fell to his knees and drew the blade out of his pocket. He wiped the rain, which was falling harder now, from his face.

In thicket the Legion had taught him to depend, not on sight, but on sound. An enemy could approach unseen, but never unheard. Black closed his eyes, and listened into the silence.

At first it was a low rustle, like a deer stepping through the foliage. Black tried to fix the sound, to judge if the follower was above him on the slope, or below him close to the path.

From his boyhood he recalled the Celtic myth of the trees that became warriors, and aided the hero in battle. *May they gather around me now.*

The soft patter of the leaves drew closer, drew level. His pursuer was below him on the slope. Black opened his eyes. Slivers of grey light lay finger-like on the forest floor.

He could see the follower, a dark shape on the edge of the path where the soft grass would muffle his footfall. He was moving slowly, and had not seen his quarry crouched behind a broad oak.

Black moved his weight on to one knee and raised the knife above his head.

He thought of Algeria, a humid night in 1962 when he had killed an Arab rebel with the knife. The man had opened his mouth in a silent scream. Black carried the image in his mind. The two men were bonded forever.

Before Black could move, the stillness was shattered by a loud snap that was crystal clear in the natural amphitheatre of the forest basin.

Down at the edge of the path, the follower screamed and fell backwards, his hand clutching frantically at his right leg.

Black had not thrown the knife. Confused, he froze as the dark figure fell.

Fighting to comprehend what had happened, he lunged forward at the bulky, screaming shape on the ground. The wordless squeals sounded like a hare in the teeth of a fox.

Black pinned the follower's upper arms to the ground. A tinkling, cracking sound formed a bizarre counterpoint to the piercing screams.

He could see the pale skin of the man's hands in the growing light. He was not armed, but his fingers were fastened on an arc of rusted steel at the base of his right calf.

A poacher's snare had crunched his anklebone, and cut into the sinew above his heel.

Black glanced down at a pool of white disks tumbling out of the tunic pocket, like coins spilling to the ground. In the light, he saw they were a dozen yellow seashells.

Black pulled back the follower's cap, and looked into the face contorted with pain.

His eyes met the blank stare of the simple man he had seen at the window, staring into the Mulroy Bay Hotel.

The follower was Hobo.

*****

Black loosened his grip on the childlike figure, whose eyes were filled with tears from the pain in his leg. He leaned down, braced himself, and heaved apart the snare.

Then he shifted the man's bulk on to his shoulder, for the walk to the house.

Back at the house, Mary Gallagher had seen them coming and was waiting in the doorway.

"God bless him," she said, once they had settled Hobo on the sofa, and bound his wound. "Doctor Kavanagh will take a look at that ankle.

"Hobo wanders the village, he's like a tomcat marking his territory. But there's no harm in him. He drives Father McLaughlin to distraction, he's forever lifting those shells from the flowerbeds at the church. He wouldn't have been following you. In fact, probably didn't even know who you were," she said.

"Just last week he came home soaked to the skin. He had fallen into a stagnant pool at the quarry. He might have drowned. It's so sad, when you think of the family he came from," said Mary Gallagher. She nodded solemnly, as Donegal women do when unveiling a dark secret.

"He's one of the McCabes from up at the big house. They have money. A fish factory down near Killybegs. Relatives, would you believe, of James Foley."

She lifted the phone to ring Doctor Kavanagh. "But they don't look after Hobo. His being ... not all there, I mean. He has his cottage all right, but it's falling down, and they don't lift a finger."

Black walked down to the scullery, and untied his muddy boots. He made a mental note to send someone to look over Hobo's cottage.

In the hall, Mary Gallagher had phoned for the doctor, and was already telling the morning's excitement to the receptionist at the surgery.

Black thought of London, and wondered who else might be listening on the line.

13

VENICE, MARCH 2005

Vaporetto No. 1 steamed gently under the Ponti dell'Accademia and nosed towards the mouth of the Grand Canal. Venice was awash with colour, and a veil of golden sunlight was drifting over the brackish waters of the Bacino di San Marco.

The younger of the two men in dark suits was engrossed in the tabloid newspaper he had bought an hour earlier at the main railway station. His top shirt button was undone, and the ragged knot in his tie was stranded two inches below his chin.

Robert and Deano had come to Venice.

"You won't believe it, Robert-o," said Deano. A solitary gull squealed and rose from the handrail, as if startled by the broad Belfast accent.

"Some minister from the Free State calling Nor'n Ireland 'a police state within a police state'. Cheeky bastard. Must have taken them hours to come up with that one."

The other suit did not reply. He was gazing at the hazy domes of Santa Maria della Salute on the bank of the canal.

Deano lowered his newspaper, and looked at his watch. "Nearly two hours to get in from the hotel. Could we not have got somewhere more central, Roberto?"

Although his name was Robert, he had been dubbed 'Monsignore Roberto' by the concierge of the small hotel on the outskirts of the city, where they had stayed the previous night.

Roberto still did not look round. "The website didn't say it was far out. It said 'offering respite from the hustle and bustle of the city centre'."

Deano followed his companion's gaze to the domed building opposite. "Too many churches in this bloody town for my liking," he muttered, flapping open his paper again. He felt awkward in the suit, and he was tired of the older man treating him like an apprentice.

The gothic fassade of the Palazzo Ducale glided into view, resplendent on the edge of the riverbank. Roberto flipped open his tourist guide, and read aloud: *"Palazzo Ducale. The Ducal Palace ... pink Veronese marble atop a fretwork of loggias and arcades in white Istrian stone."*

Deano rose with Robert as they prepared to alight.

"I can't see any arcades. Maybe they're only open in the summer," he muttered.

"But you have to hand it to them. It's dead spotless," he continued, folding his newspaper and squinting sideways at the same time. "Clean as a whistle. If this was Belfast, there'd be graffiti all over the place."

A distinguished-looking gentleman in a red cardigan, standing in front of them, smiled an indulgent smile. He leaned backward to take in the full façade of the *Palazzo*, and pointed his handycam towards it.

Roberto looked at Deano with distaste, asking himself at the same time if he was being unreasonable. It was not the boy's fault. Joining the terrorist movement in Belfast hardly required an intimate knowledge of the Italian baroque.

Nonetheless, since they had met at Belfast International Airport the previous day, he been worried. Deano was too brash. This assignment was Roberto's chance to convince the leadership that he was 'management' material. Last thing he needed was some young upstart screwing it up.

Deano did not know that, were he to endanger the operation, Roberto had clearance to snap his neck and drop him in the lagoon. Roberto did not know that, were the operation to fail, another operative was in Venice who would do the same to him. Making this connection was of Priority A importance. Screw-ups were not an option.

It occurred to Roberto that perhaps Deano should take a walk, while he went to the meeting alone. But no. He had warned Deano to keep his mouth shut and, besides, their contact was expecting two of them.

The vaporetto sidled up to the wall of the Riva degli Schiavoni at San Zaccaria Pièta. Deano twisted his newspaper into a roll, and pressed it down into a litter bin.

"Do up the tie," said Roberto, "or they won't let you through the door."

It was sixteen minutes to ten. All was running perfectly to schedule.

In five minutes, they would be in the Hotel Danieli.

*****

CHALFONT ST. GILES, ENGLAND

Sir Anthony Cathcart was working from home.

He was in the garden pruning his roses, when his mobile rang. He peeled off a pink glove and flipped the phone open. It was a call he was expecting. "Cathcart, hello?"

"Hello, Sir. They are now arriving at the hotel. I will have live video for you, starting in about in about five minutes," said the distinguished-looking man in the red cardigan.

Sir Anthony popped his phone back into the chest pocket of his gardening smock.

He shouted towards the house. "Jean, would you mind powering up my laptop for a live video conference? I'll be there in two minutes."

As his personal assistant for over twenty years, Jean was privy to all his legal activities, and also the occasional assassination.

"Certainly," called Jean, "and I'll put the kettle on."

*****

Roberto and Deano gazed breathlessly around the foyer of the ancestral palace of the Dandolo family.

They stepped through large marble columns flanked by tall palms, and looked at their reflections in a veneer floor buffed to perfection. To their left, a staircase with a red carpet led to a mezzanine with a long balcony that overlooked the hall. From there, a white stone balustrade with a vaulted canopy led to another floor above.

Roberto could see that no-one was seated in the lobby area. There was time yet. It was only six minutes to ten.

Deano looked at the exquisite chandeliers suspended over the lobby, and wondered what they were worth.

A bookish, swarthy gentleman appeared on the balcony above, in a white linen suit that was surprisingly unseasonal for early March. He was wearing a cream panama hat and, as he descended the stairs, he produced a pair of gold spectacles from inside his jacket, which he positioned fussily on his nose.

He ambled directly across the hall, looking neither to the right or the left, and placed his briefcase delicately on a table in the corner. An attentive waiter approached, a white napkin folded over his forearm. A brief exchange of words, and the waiter bowed politely and scurried into the labyrinth of the *palazzo*.

Neither Roberto nor Deano took any notice of the man in the red cardigan from the *vaporetto* taking position at the back of the balcony. He was just another tourist with a videocam.

Through the fronds of the hanging palm, Roberto observed the man in white as he opened his briefcase, and laid a leather document pouch, a fountain pen and a small étui on the marble top.

The box was the agreed signal. "Wait here," Roberto said to Deano. He walked at a measured pace to a brightly-lit jewellery showcase, close to where the man in white was sitting.

Back at the hanging palm, Deano peered at the glittering watches hanging in the display, and wondered what they were worth.

Roberto looked at the reflection of the marble tabletop in the glass front of the display case. 'A sandalwood étui with a scrimshaw carving of a Chinese pagoda', his instructions had said. From his schooldays, he seemed to remember 'pagoda' as being a Chinese boat. 'Scrimshaw' he had looked up in the dictionary. Now he could see the fine intaglio of yellowed ivory on the ochre lid. There had been a small error of detail. It was a Chinese house.

"Mister Alberto."

"Ah Monsignore Robert. Welcome to Venice. The weather is ... splendid." Alberto hitched up his glasses on his nose and half-rose to his feet. He extended his hand.

Roberto gestured to Deano to approach. "My associate, Mr. Denton Small." Deano shook Alberto's hand awkwardly and mumbled an indecipherable greeting. He stood wringing his fingers in the uneasy pause that followed. He should have kept the newspaper, it would have been something to carry.

Alberto broke the silence.

"Knowing that you would be on time, I have taken the liberty of ordering tea. It will arrive ... presently. Please sit."

Deano's discomfiture indicated that Roberto was the senior figure, and Alberto shifted his chair slightly towards him.

"Have you been here already a day or two, Mr. Roberto?" he said in a rich Italian accent. "It would be a scandal were you to depart without absorbing some of the flavours of Venezia."

"We have already seen the Grand Canal this morning, Mr. Alberto." replied Roberto. "The city is fabulous. So much heritage. Impressive even for those of us who come, it has been said, from a country that pays ... *too much* attention to history."

Deano was now outside the discussion. His mind was beginning to wander. He examined the objects on the table and his eye fell on Alberto's fountain pen. He wondered how much it was worth.

At that moment, the waiter brought a plump Russian samovar with an intricate blue delft tap, three snow-white bone china cups with the shield motif of Hotel Danieli, and a small ramekin of assorted sugarlumps.

In deference to the British visitors, there was also a small jug of milk.

Alberto sipped the tea, and replaced his cup on its saucer. He pushed his glasses up on his nose, moving to the business at hand. "Gentlemen, I have only good news for you this morning. After long deliberations, my employer has agreed to accept this commission, assuming, of course, that the terms provided to you can be met. I must say, I was somewhat surprised. In recent years, my employer has confined any work of this nature to Italy."

Roberto smiled, and rummaged in his briefcase. "That is good news," he said, clipping his words for the benefit of the foreigner.

"This envelope contains all the information your employer will require. We will deposit an initial $2.5 million in his Swiss bank account, as requested. For additional security, that will be routed through one of our companies in Panama."

Alberto did not challenge Roberto's assumption that his employer was a man. All clients did so. It had been a source of mild amusement to himself, and Maria Gandelli, in the past.

Alberto listened intently, as Roberto continued. "The money will be quite untracable. The other half will follow, by the same route, after the contract has been fulfilled.

"Our only concern is the timing of the project. As you know, there is an element of urgency. We need this done in weeks, rather than months."

Roberto looked at Alberto to gauge his reaction. The Italian touched his glasses again, but remained impassive. It appeared that he did not know the answer. Perhaps he needed a more direct question.

"Can your employer service this contract so quickly, Mr. Alberto? If necessary we can assist him, when he arrives in Ireland. In the company of local accents, he is less likely to be noticed."

Alberto smiled and shook his head. "Thank you, but my employer has a strict rule. He does not meet with clients, nor their agents. He also insists on fulfilling the termination order alone, at a time and by a method of his own choosing. All of this will remain private information. You will next be aware of him when you read news of a tragic death in your morning paper. By that time, my employer will be back in Italy.

"Please do not worry, Mr. Roberto. My employer has never been known to fail."

Roberto smiled, and placed his cup in its saucer. He turned to Deano.

"Deano, perhaps we should spend a few hours walking, before our flight."

Alberto collected his items and flapped closed his leather pouch.

"May I recommend the Basilica di San Marco, and of course the Palazzo Ducale, just here on the bay," said Alberto, rising to his feet with an elegant gesture.

"Everyone should see Tintoretto's 'Paradise' before they die. It is in the main hall of the *Palazzo*, where the Great Council of Venice used to meet."

"We are al-ways up for a good paint-ing," said Deano, mocking Roberto's clear pronounciation.

"Ah but Mr. Deano, this is not just a painting. It is a ... what is it in English, *una pittura murale*. It is a mural!" Alberto laughed, gathering up his briefcase.

"It comes from the sixteenth century. You will be impressed, I promise. So well executed."

Alberto proferred his hand to both the men. "Goodbye, gentlemen. So nice to have met you." He bowed, turned, and, still grinning, walked briskly to the stairway, up to the balcony, and back towards his room.

Deano wondered if Alberto was laughing at him. He muttered under his breath."We have our own 'paintings on the wall' in Belfast too, Mr. Al-ber-to.

"And a few of those guys were well-executed, too."

*****

Sir Anthony Cathcart closed his laptop and made a mental note to stay at the Hotel Danieli.

He crossed his office to a matching pair of mahogany bookcases. Between them, the Collins map of the British Isles was fixed to a cork notice board.

He took a scarlet red drawing pin from the edge of the board, and pushed it into the map in the north-west of Ireland, between Milford and Carrigart. "Ardsallagh," he whispered to himself. "Ardsallagh". The word sounded odd, from his lips, lacking the rounded 'r' of the local Irish accent.

Sir Anthony turned to the small gaming table to the left of his desk. On the botticino marble chessboard, a game was in progress.

He would have his next move for Sir Geraint, before the morning was out.

14

DUBLIN AIRPORT, A MONTH LATER

The soldier on crutches met a deafening wave of cheers as he limped into the arrivals hall of Dublin Airport.

Two small figures darted towards him, skipping around the legs of the spectators as if running through a forest. He embraced his twin girls, blonde hair flowing over their lemon dresses.

Behind them ran a tall woman in jeans and a white blouse, excusing herself to right and left as she pushed to keep up with her children. As she reached the soldier, she handed him a pint of creamy stout.

Battle. Exile. Family. An injured soldier coming home.

The roar of the crowd rose to a deafening pitch.

*****

At the front of the arrivals hall, Darkey Byrne was propped on his mop, drying his fingers on his overalls.

"God knows what they're doing sending our lads to Kosovo, as true as God. In my time, they went no further than Finner Camp. It's think local, kill global, these days, Nora."

His companion smiled, and pressed the trigger-gun of green disinfectant against her apron. The once-white badge on her pinafore bore the legend: 'Cleaning Staff – Nora Geoghegan'.

"Blood is thicker than water, Darkey. You're always glad to see your own flesh and blood home safe." She dropped her washrag neatly into the metal bucket. "There'll be some celebrations in the pubs of Tallaght tonight."

Darkey Byrne drew up to the fullness of his five feet and two inches. *The pubs of Tallaght.* "They'd be safer back in Kosovo."

The doors slid open again. Another pair of demob-happy soldiers trundled through. A floppy yellow rabbit swayed on the luggage trolley, atop a mountain of green gunnysacks. Another child ran forward. The applause began again.

Maria Gandelli had been lucky. The military plane had touched down fifteen minutes ahead of the passenger flight from Milan to Dublin. No-one noticed the elegant Italian in dark glasses, looking down to avoid the CCTV.

She had turned right, and melted away into the crowd.

*****

DONEGAL, THE NEXT DAY

Maria swore as she steered into the yard of the Metropole Hotel in Donegal Town.

She had left the Holiday Inn Dublin Airport at 5pm. The road north had taken three hours in the rented Fiat Punto. She was not used to small cars, and the need for a low profile was wearing her down. A twenty-minute flight to the helipad in the grounds would have been more her style.

She cut the engine. It was eight o'clock. A percussive jingle announced the evening news. "Continuing sectarian violence is the major obstacle to kick-starting the Peace Process by the end of the summer, according to the Taoiseach, James Foley. Speaking after his meeting today at Downing Street, Mr. Foley said: *"This is an age of change. The outmoded attitudes of yesterday have no place in the new social order..."*

Gandelli switched off the radio. She had no interest in politics, especially the tangled mess that was politics in Ireland. Right now, she was more interested in food. She wondered if a late dinner would disturb her sleep.

The surly receptionist made the decision for her. "No hot food on room service after 8pm, madam. You can go into the restaurant, if you like, or we can do you up a sandwich."

The receptionist eyed her through a pair of thick glasses. She was dressed casually, baggy sweatshirt and jeans, little make-up and no jewellery. Just how a tourist or a travelling rep would look. But it was obvious this was no saleswoman. Even when dressing down, Maria Gandelli could not conceal her natural elegance.

The receptionist sniffed, as plain women do when confronted by beauty. She looked Gandelli up and down again, and handed over the key.

From the foyer, Gandelli could see four plump businessmen laughing loudly in the restaurant. Men who would notice a woman dining alone. No point in attracting attention. A ploughman's lunch upstairs would have to do.

In the room, she flipped open the orange dossier and looked at the photograph of Tom Black. There were also several press clippings from the *Belfast Telegraph* and *Irish Times*. Black emerging from No. 10. Black on the steps of the Irish Department of Foreign Affairs. Black and Foley through the window of a limo.

Alberto's notes were neatly typed in Italian.

"Residence: Ardsallagh, between Milford and Carrigart, Co. Donegal, Ireland.

Current residents of house: Tom Black and Jacques de Vries. Both ex-Legion, proficient in gun-handling and self-defence. Black also proficient with the knife. Unknown what weapons are present in the house.

No reason to believe that target is aware of contract, but utmost caution and element of surprise essential.

Home alarmed, but no security cameras. Alarm will be disabled 12 hours prior to deadline. Main hall remains active so that alarm appears to function normally.

Black currently attending negotiations with Irish prime minister in London. Return expected Saturday 14th."

Maria Gandelli opened her jewellery box and slipped on a quarter of a million dollars of precious stones. Two rings: one ruby, the other amethyst. *A low profile should not go too far.* She felt like a beautiful woman again. *Una bella donna.*

The bejewelled fingers closed the orange dossier.

As usual, Alberto had done his job very well.

*****

LOUGH SWILLY, COUNTY DONEGAL, 3.14AM

They called it Lough Swilly: the lake of shadows. In the moonlight, the blue and green strips that shimmered on the surface revealed the uneven sea bed beneath. It was not a lake at all, but a salt water bay to the west of the Inishowen Peninsula, the northernmost tip of Ireland.

Callaghan's hands were shaky with nerves as he rowed the small boat round the head at Portsalon, and struck out for the promontory at Father Hegarty's Rock.

The redcoats had ambushed the priest saying mass there in sixteen hundred and nine. He had fled on to the lake, in a boat no bigger than Callaghan's own. They lured him back with a promise of safety. Then, they cut off his head with their bayonets.

Callaghan was hoping for better luck. The full moon over Linsfort Strand was brighter than he would have liked. He pushed on through the silent water. The sooner this was over, the better.

The starlight glinted on the silver instrument case they had paid him five grand to deliver.

Of course, he'd have liked to know what was in the box, but for that kind of money you don't ask questions.

High in the Urris Hills to the north, a single headlight flickered. Some late-night drinker, returning to his farm. Callaghan had passed the half-way mark. Ahead, he could make out the tall figure standing at the rock, watching his progress.

He landed on a short strip of sand and, as instructed, placed his cargo in the shelter of the rock. The watcher above did not move.

Callaghan climbed back into the boat and drew on the oars. As he pulled away, the hooded figure clambered down to collect the box. Who cared what it contained. He was four months' wages the richer.

Maria Gandelli carried the silver case with the Beretta handgun back up to the car, and fired up the engine. She drove the first fifty yards at walking speed, with no lights. Then she fired up the full beam, and sped away.

*****

Mary Gallagher was cross.

Lee and Gerard from HomeSecure Alarms had arrived as she was kneading dough, and she had smudged her polished brass doorhandles in her rush to the front of the house.

"Will it take long, now?" she barked, wiping the last specks of dough into the folds of her apron. She would tolerate their routine check of the alarms, but she would not, she decided, offer them a cup of tea.

"We'll have it done in two shakes," said Lee, the clean-cut one in the neat blue overall. Mary Gallagher did not notice that he had no logo on his workwear.

"And where have you come up from?" she said. "You're not local."

"We've come down from Derry, madam. We service quite a few alarms here in the area," said Lee. He was hung over from the night before, but managed to force a grin.

Mary Gallagher harrumphed, and bustled off to turn down her oven.

Gerry had set up his ladder in the lounge. He listened intently to the exchange of words in the hall. As long as they were talking, Mary Gallagher was paying no attention to him.

He screwed the lid off the small yellow tin, and slipped it into his breast pocket. He smeared a film of petroleum jelly over the front of the motion sensor, disabling it in a way that was invisible to the eye. He would do the same in the rooms across the hall.

Climbing down, he checked that Mary Gallagher was not returning, and fell to his knees at the french windows. With a pliers he clipped the cable to the circuit breaker on the window pane. He bared two of the four wires, and twisted them into one, recreating the circuit. He sealed the join with a strip of black insulating tape, and tucked the loop of wire against the skirting board, flush with the carpet.

Whoever they were, they could now enter from the french windows. And with the sensor blinded by the film of jelly, they could move freely through the room.

Gerry nodded politely as they lugged their aluminium steps back through the hall. Mary Gallagher held the door for them. Now she could get back to her bread.

Lee wiped the perspiration from his eyes, as he tossed the

toolbox into the back of the plain red van. The whole operation had taken only twelve minutes. It had been the longest twelve minutes of his life.

Thank God she hadn't offered them a cup of tea.

*****

At precisely 10am next morning, Maria Gandelli slipped her ruby and amethyst rings off and dropped them into a small casket. She pressed it to the back of the glove compartment of the blue Fiat Punto. She was wearing sunglasses, and her hair was tied back.

She had brought the car to a halt at the back of Cratlagh Wood. The drive had taken over an hour, and in the last 100 yards, the Fiat's suspension had rattled her bones. It was hardly designed for off-road.

The grey chimneys of Ardsallagh peeped through the trees 150 yards to her left. From a satchel on the front seat she took a Carl Zeiss sports binoculars and her mobile phone.

At the back of the car, she changed from shoes to rubber boots, and pushed through the thicket to within forty yards of the outhouse behind the main building.

Keeping low, she focussed the binoculars on a red Ford Fiesta sitting at a diagonal to the front facade of the house. Everything told her it was Mary Gallagher's car: the small crucifix dangling from the driver's mirror, the two weeks of mud on the body, and the orange cat spread-eagled in the back window, a present from her grandchildren.

Gandelli punched a number into her mobile. No need to attempt an Irish accent. Mary Gallagher would not challenge her perfect American.

"Hello. Ardsallagh House."

"Hi, good morning. This is the Donegal Oil Company. We'll have a vehicle delivering in your area tomorrow. We wondered if you'd like to check your tank?"

For the second time in two days, Mary Gallagher had been disturbed at her housework. "No. Thank you. If we need oil, we'll ring you. Next week."

"That would mean a ten-euro surcharge for delivery, whereas if you take advantage of tomorrow's lorry, delivery would be free."

Now, saving money was a different matter. Waste not, want not, they said in Carrigart, and Mary Gallagher was a good country woman with good country sense.

"I'll have to go out to the yard to check."

"Thank you, ma'am," said the polite American. "If you are speaking on a cordless phone, take it with you. I can direct you where to look on the tank."

"No, I have to put the receiver down. I'll not be a minute," said the housekeeper.

Gandelli made a mental note: the house phone was a landline, not a mobile.

Mary Gallagher scowled at the heavy sky through the kitchen window. There was rain coming, but in Donegal, there was always rain coming. She opened the back door, and trudged down to the main outhouse.

Behind her, Maria Gandelli was already across the yard, pressed against the ornate French windows that faced into the wood. She was pleased to see the driveway was hard mud. It would make less noise than gravel.

She peered into the lounge, then raised the digital camera and clicked three photos – left, right and centre. It was all over even before Mary Gallagher had located the oil gauge.

By the time the housekeeper picked up the phone again, Maria Gandelli was back in her car.

"Eight hundred litres, that's about half full. Now, I'll not order more oil without asking the owner, and he isn't here at present. I can check with him tonight. You can ring again tomorrow, if you want."

Alberto's timing for Black's return was confirmed.

*****

In the bedroom at the Metropole Hotel, Maria flicked the remote and tossed a handful of brochures for Donegal tweeds on to the bed. Officially, she was a fashion designer, in Ireland to collect ideas for her winter ranges.

Irish tv offered a mixture of political debate and mindless home makeover shows. One channel was showing a profile of a musical instrument maker from County Waterford. She was a fan of the famous crystal, so she let it run for background noise, and poured herself a glass of white burgundy from the ice bucket. French wine was acceptable, when she was not home in Italy.

The camera was uploading to the laptop. Beside it stood a yellow legal pad and a fountain pen. Making a sketch of a room fixed the layout in her mind. Having a mental picture could be crucial, when moving in darkness.

The first photo showed the left side of the room, towards the rear of the house. She had been unable to use flash through the glass. She opened Photoshop and raised the brightness until the candlesticks on the fireplace were clearly visible.

She stared at the screen and frowned. Something was bothering her in the images of the drawing room, but it was something she could not pin down.

She reached aside to rummage in her bag.

For the first time in a month, she wanted a cigarette.

*****

CARRIGART, THE NEXT NIGHT

Maria Gandelli rounded the bend on the Milford Road at 2.56am, and approached Ardsallagh house for the last time.

She dipped her lights as she pulled left into the side-road, and nosed 150 yards into the cover of the wood.

The road was Tom Black's creation; it had been built with Ardsallagh a year earlier. In time, it would make a perfect 'lover's lane'. For tonight, however, the wood was deserted.

She lifted the silver instrument case on to the passenger seat, snapped up the clips, and lifted the cover. It had struck her before: no matter how mild an evening, a .22 Beretta was always cold to the touch.

The pistol was small calibre, but two shots to the head, and the target was just as dead. The Beretta made no messy exit wounds, useful if a body needed to be moved.

Ardsallagh House was dark. Black's Chrysler was not yet in sight. Alberto had confirmed that Mary Gallagher did not spend nights in the house.

In thirty seconds Gandelli was across the yard, through the french windows, and into the lounge.

Her mind wandered to an appointment with her ad agency in five days in Rome. She smiled at her own nonchalance. Every contract was the same. Even at the kill, her pulse never rose above sixty.

She lowered herself into the leather chair facing the door, laid the Beretta by her side, and settled in to wait.

It was 3.12am.

*****

At four in the morning, the roar of a diesel jeep seems three times louder than during the day.

The headlamps of the Chrysler swept the trees in the drive like a lighthouse, as it pulled in from the road. Black had made his return.

Maria Gandelli's mouth was dry. She should have brought a tonic water.

Her gloved hand slid around the Beretta. When it sank to the bottom of the bay tomorrow, it would be the fourteenth she had disposed of in twelve years. She wondered if it made her a special customer.

The jeep pulled round and parked front-on to the french windows, flooding the room with light. She was out of sight in the armchair, when the light hit the picture that was hanging in the hearth. Her heart stopped.

Black entered at the back of the building, coming into the kitchen. The clack of leather shoes on liscannor stone echoed along the hall. He flicked on the light.

At the sound of the door closing, Gandelli stood up and placed her left hand on the marble mantelpiece. Her eyes remained fixed on the photo in the hearth. The Beretta slipped out of her hand and fell softly on to the carpet.

Black walked to the farmhouse table inside the kitchen door. He put down his briefcase and the copy of the London 'Times' he had purchased in the airport in Carrickfin.

On top of the newspaper he placed the car keys and the holstered handgun he had carried since the incident with Hobo in the forest.

He opened the fridge, poured a double gin and tonic, and cursed as he saw he was out of sliced lemons.

When he turned, Maria Gandelli was standing in the doorway. She had removed the gloves, but held the Beretta in her left hand. Black stood motionless. He was within reach of his gun. The tumbler sounded loud as a cannon, as he placed it on the formica top.

Gandelli stepped forward, reached to the table, placed her hand over his holster, and carried it back to the doorway.

This was no soldier, but Black knew better than to underestimate her. She had to be a professional. She had to be good. She was waiting for him in his own house, after all. Those manicured fingernails had fired a Beretta before.

Black's breathing quickened, and he broke into a sweat.

"Who are you?"

"I was sent here to kill you."

"If you'd wanted to kill me, I'd be dead by now." Black flexed his fingers, and gauged how far he was from the knife drawer. "So. You want to talk."

Maria Gandelli turned, and Black saw she had the picture in her hand. She reached forward and laid it on the table.

He gazed down at the faces of Mary the barmaid and four GI's in the Grand Central Bar in 1944.

"Who are the people in the photograph?" she said, still pointing the Beretta. The last time Black had had a gun pointed at him, an Arab was behind it. But this was different. Her tone was even and cool, not threatening. He cleared his throat.

"Mary Black, the barmaid, was my mother. I believe the sailor to her right was my late father. She told me his name was Joseph."

His thoughts were racing, tumbling. *Why am I telling an armed stranger about my family?*

It didn't matter that she had a gun. Black suddenly realised he had lost his fear of death.

"He is not your late father. He's alive, and living in retirement in Rome," said Maria Gandelli.

Black pressed his fingers to his forehead. He struggled to make sense of the situation.

"How do you know this?" It was the best he could do.

Gandelli paused. She wished she had another cigarette.

"Joe Gandelli is my father too."

She placed the two pistols on the table, and walked away from them.

"In Italy, we don't kill family. *Il sangue non è acqua.* Blood is thicker than water."

Maria Gandelli leaned back against the counter, and folded her arms.

"Now that we are on the same side, aren't you going to offer me a drink?"

15

St. James' Keep, Gower Peninsula

Sir Geraint Welles swore as he fumbled under the sofa cushion.

Yet again, he had confused the ringing of his cellphone with the alarm of his Palm organiser. Too many gadgets these days. He had always been more of a telex man.

He found the remote, silenced the tv, and punched the answer button on the phone. He pushed his glasses up on the bridge of his nose.

"Yes, this is he. Welles. What is it?

His face remained stony as he listened to the anonymous message. "I see. Thank you."

Welles stood up, and walked out through the french windows on to the west balcony of St. James' Keep. The moon was bright. White surf was breaking on the rocks below.

He raised his cellphone again. This time it was to dial a London number.

In his apartment in Pimlico, Sir Anthony Cathcart ignored the ringing phone. He was concentrating on working late with Jayne Williams, an ambitious young colleague from the administration department, whose head, at that moment, was bobbing rhythmically in his lap.

Miss Williams was a horsey girl. The jodhpurs she wore to the office, together with the rest of her clothes, were scattered over the russet pile carpet picked specially for the apartment by Cathcart's ex-wife, Natalie.

She had left him a year previously. Their marriage had been the victim, not of his occasional departures from fidelity, but of twenty-three years of his punishing work regime at the Ministry.

Miss Williams from administration laboured on. Cathcart's eyes scanned the roof. He sighed. It was looking a little tired. It needed repainted. These things had always been seen to by Natalie. With her gone, domestic concerns had been somewhat ignored.

Thoughts of Natalie reminded Cathcart of a poster he had found amusing. It had been an ad for ketchup.

"Give him a little taste of what he gets downtown."

He had found the sexual innuendo amusing. And dear Natalie, bless her, never had. Given him a taste of what he could get downtown, that is. Miss Williams, on the other hand, was the very model of earnest effort and efficiency.

Ten minutes later, when they had concluded their meeting, Cathcart checked his voicemail for the missed call.

Immediately, he rang Sir Geraint back.

"Ah Cathcart, good of you to answer so promptly. I have been contacted by our associates."

Welles was standing by the bookshelves at the long window of the Keep's drawing room, looking at the game in progress on his marble chessboard.

"It would appear that ... queen has taken knight."

Cathcart was seated in his bathroom, on the edge of the jacuzzi, his left hand cupped around his genitals to shield them from the cold porcelain. He knew that Welles was not referring to chess. Welles had been informed that the hit on Tom Black had been fulfilled by Maria Gandelli.

He gazed at the milk-white bottom of Miss Williams six feet away, wobbling as she slooshed mouthwash at the sink.

He snapped closed his phone.

"Check and ... checkmate, Mr. Black."

*****

"Jacques."

Maria Gandelli curled her long fingers around the glass of gin. Black was talking past her. Looking through her.

In the hall, the kitchen light glinted on the barrel of a rifle as de Vries emerged from the shadows.

It seemed that her half-brother shared her instinct for self-preservation.

"So you knew I was coming."

Black was smug. "I'm afraid we did. It was Mary. The housekeeper. She's Special Services. A ruthless, trained killer."

De Vries laughed nervously at Black's joke. It did nothing to dispel the tension in the kitchen.

Gandelli remained stoney-faced. It irked her to be outfoxed by a former soldier. If this was haughtiness on her part, she did not care. She was the specialist, and Black a mere infantryman.

This was also no time for levity. If she had moved on Black, de Vries would have blown her away.

"Special Services. Unlikely," she said, fishing for a more substantial explanation. Black decided to put her out of her misery.

"We found the gel on the alarm monitors," he said.

He turned to de Vries. Better to clue him in on the situation. "Jacques, it appears that my nemesis and I share more than a taste for gin and tonic. We also share a blood line. This," he said with a quizzical look, "is Miss Maria Gandelli. It appears we share the same father."

De Vries shook her hand with a perplexed expression.

"My connection to Mr. Black is an unfortunate circumstance which cannot be denied, Mister de Vries. However, it would appear to have saved his ... what is the term over here? His ... bacon."

Black lifted de Vries' rifle.

"On the contrary, Miss Gandelli," he said, peering along the sleek barrel.

"It would appear to have saved yours."

*****

Black poured coffee for three and looked at his watch. It was 8.30am, and they had regrouped in the kitchen after an uneasy and fitful sleep.

"Miss Gandelli, how long before your clients realise that they have been misled about the completion of the contract?" It would be some time before he would feel natural using her first name.

"I sent a message that you were dead at half past four this morning. We probably have three days. Maybe four. They wanted you removed before the Dublin summit at the weekend."

"And if they figure it out before then, will they have a back-up?

Someone else ready to move on us?" said Black.

"Mister Black, I do not even know who 'they' are. But I would doubt it. Vendors in my business are unprepared for such situations, due to the fact that vendors such as I rarely..." The phrase was sticking in her throat... "renegue on a contract."

"Then let's be cautious. Assume we have just 48 hours instead of twice that. Do we go underground, try to identify them and expose them, before they get to us?"

"Exposing them would be pointless, Mister Black. There has been only indirect contact. They are faceless, and if we cannot prove our accusations, we cannot expose them in time to stop the contract. I'm afraid we have only one option. We must remove them from the game."

Black was uneasy. Gandelli was, after all, proposing a bloodbath. And a very public one, at that.

"These people are probably high profile, not some penpushers out in the provinces. Perhaps we should be less ... trigger-happy, Miss Gandelli."

She winced. It was the second dent in her professional pride in twenty-four hours.

"Mister Black, do not attempt to give me a moral lecture. We are both professional killers. At opposite ends of the market, that is all. You are K-Mart, and I am ... Versace. You kill Arabs in the desert for pennies. I kill their leaders for five million dollars a shot. And I, incidentally, provide the greater public service."

She flicked her hair. Finally, they understood each other. "Now. I have something to show you."

Gandelli laid a plain white envelope on the table. Black opened it, and drew out four photos. They were blurred, and monochrome, but he knew Venice and he immediately recognised the foyer of the hotel.

"My agent sent them to me on the web," Gandelli continued.

"Stills from CCTV. It's all rather 'James Bond', I'm afraid, but he likes to have insurance. He said they had Irish accents. Friends of yours, Mister Black?"

The barb in her comment was not lost on him, but Black ignored it. He could see she was irked at not having foreseen his trap, and he was enjoying her professional pique.

"These, Miss Gandelli, are the type of friends you don't need. If they're Irish, they're probably from one of the terrorist organisations here.

"I don't know them. But I know someone who will."

*****

THE SEGMENT BAR, BELFAST. 2.45PM

Black struggled to adapt his eyes to the smoky blur of the shabby and dilapidated drinking den. Worn carpets, the sour stench of spilled lager, soggy cigarette-butts in battered tin bowls.

He was in the heartland of loyalist Belfast, and this was the stale residue of thirty years of spilled ale and hatred.

Chocca Pearson was sitting at the front of the bar, like a guard dog at the door. He leered at the tall frame of Maria Gandelli as she stepped through the door. He glanced at Black, with no nod of recognition.

"Chocca. This is Maria Gandelli, a guest from Italy. Perhaps you could entertain her for a few minutes while I have a word with Jimmy," said Black.

Chocca tried to look taller. He kept his eyes on Maria. "My pleasure. You'll find Mister Williamson at the back. In the V.I.P. area," he said, grinning at Maria.

"Come this way, Miss Gandelli."

Chocca led her to one side, to a small booth by the window. Without asking, he ordered her a gin and tonic and a pint for himself. The drinks were brought.

"Well. All the way from Italy. We don't tend to get many tourists in here," said Chocca. He was sitting too close. He could smell a sweet waft of very expensive perfume on Maria Gandelli's hair. She could smell the last pint on his breath. He moved closer still. His thigh made contact with hers.

Chocca was an optimist with women. He was inclined to think that, if he hadn't been physically pushed away, he was making progress.

"I am Sardinian, actually. Do you know Sardinia?" said Gandelli.

Her sarcastic tone did not register with Chocca.

"Sardinia is an island off Italy. Let me tell you about Sardinian girls," Gandelli said.

She was making eye contact with Chocca. She was smiling coquettishly. She placed her left hand on his thigh. Chocca was not believing his luck. Her hand inched higher.

"Sardinian girls learn to castrate goats at age five. With a single cut."

Chocca sat bolt upright. He swallowed hard, suddenly conscious of the soft package between his legs. He snapped them shut, involuntarily.

Maria Gandelli had withdrawn her hand. There was no point in breaking a nail. Chocca had got the message.

Black spotted Jimmy Williamson sitting on his own at a plastic table near the back, like a fat king on a throne. No business folder this time, no self-iron shirt, no crisp tie.

This was where Williamson could relax. Home territory. This was where he had won his stripes.

His apprentice years had not been pretty. In The Segment in the 1970s, the rules of civilisation did not apply.

An angry crowd, drunken and bloated with beer and bigotry, had roared their approval when he dragged in a woman who had been involved with a Catholic, and shaved off her hair in the middle of the bar.

It became known that, if a bullet had to be put in the head of a suspected informer, Williamson was your man.

Jimmy Williamson had been, as they say in Belfast, a 'bad article'.

But he was older now. Some said he had mellowed. He was embracing the political way.

That was why Black had brought him to Ardsallagh. And today was payback time. It was time to see how much goodwill had come from a shared bottle of Irish whiskey, and a walk on a Donegal beach.

On the road to Belfast, Black had tried to phone ahead to Williamson, but failed to make contact. His arrival was not expected, and Williamson was unprepared.

Williamson did not rise from the plastic table to greet him. Black did not expect it. On his home patch, there was only so far that he could go. The Shankill Road was only round the corner. This, Black reflected with an uncomfortable shudder, was the heart of darkness.

If Williamson was shocked to see Black, he did not show it.

"Well, Mister B. You're about a hundred miles and a hundred years from home, in here." Away from the soft-spoken murmur of the conference table, Black saw, for the first time, the raw thug in Williamson's eyes. It was an animal, and it was just below the surface.

"You'd better have a drink."

Black thought of the Legion again, and of the code of conduct of their adversaries among the Arabs. When fanatics made a gesture of hospitality, it was unwise to refuse.

Behind Williamson's head, he eyed a tattered poster for Scottish lager held up by yellowed strips of sticky tape.

"I'll have a pint of lager. Is there a place where we can talk in private?"

Williamson smiled. His teeth seemed sharp behind the twisted grin. "Aye, I'd as soon we were out of sight, as well."

He turned to his cronies, four beer-bellied skinheads lined along the bar. "Twenty years ago, his sort wouldn't have been seen dead in here, eh lads?"

"They would not, Jimmy."

"But they'd have been seen dead out the back!"

The four burst into loud laughter at Williamson's joke. The massive shoulders jigged, the tattoos on their biceps looking like graffiti carved in a tree trunk.

Williamson snapped his fingers for the pint. He seemed relaxed enough about Black's unscheduled appearance.

He stood up, and slapped Black jovially on the shoulder.

"Don't worry, Tom. These days, we've moved on to a new age. Nowadays, as the man said, we like both kinds of music. Country *and* western."

The irony hung heavy in the air as Williamson laughed again.

The barman brought the pint, but no money changed hands. He handed it to Black, then stepped past to lead him into the darkness behind.

Black followed him through a low door that led down a stone staircase to the tap room. He flicked a switch. A bare forty-watt bulb struggled to cast a dull glow in the dank cellar. A black swastika on the once-white wall was pock-marked by the crumbling of the paint.

Williamson lit up a cigarette, and sat down on a keg. He puffed a cloud of blue mist that swirled around the bulb.

With his second drag, he visibly relaxed. Down here, they could set their own rules. Down here, they could talk.

"Jesus, Tom. You might have rung me. We could have met on neutral ground. In there, I still have a game to play." Williamson gestured back towards the club.

"Sorry, Jimmy, but this is urgent. In fact, it's an emergency – one I need like ... a hole in the head. If you know what I mean."

Williamson frowned. "Whose head are we talking about? I worry about that kind of hole every time I go out my door. It's *la condition humaine*, in my world. Comes with the patch. So ... we're talking about yourself. Either you, or Foley."

Black took a mouthful of the lager, and immediately wished he hadn't. It was cold, but it was flat. If he could, he'd have poured it away.

"It might be a more noble head altogether, Jimmy," he said, tapping with his knuckle on a beer crate stacked beside his shoulder. Williamson looked at the blazon on its side: a golden crown.

The tip of Williamson's cigarette grew to a fiery point of red. His eyes lit up with glee. He blew smoke through his nose, and chuckled loudly. He leaned forward to stub out the cigarette on the ground.

"No Tom, they wouldn't be that stupid. Once upon a time they might have thought about it, but not any more. No holes in our beloved Elisabeth R."

"Depends on who 'they' are, Jimmy. It isn't the Provos, or even these 'Continuity' boys. These are new players. I don't know who they are, but I know they don't play by our rules."

Black had no time and no choice. He decided to trust Williamson.

"They're after a Royal. Probably not the Queen, but a royal nonetheless. And they're after me as well."

Williamson had stopped smiling. He scrutinised Black's face.

Black handed over the stills from the hotel. "I need you to look at something for me."

Williamson stood to hold the photographs closer to the light. As he rose, he nudged the bulb with his head, sending the room into a flurry of rocking shadows. He scowled as he focussed on the detail in the photographs.

"Would this be Venice by any chance?"

"Spot on, Jimmy. You know your architecture."

"I know feck all about architecture. But I know this guy, his name is Robbie Matchett. Or rather, it was. They tracked him to Italy about ten days ago, and took him out. Mustn't have been too long after this photo was taken. They thought it would cause less of a fuss if they hit him abroad."

His eyes narrowed. "They were wrong."

"They?"

"His own people. It was a surprise. Some of them had high hopes for this fella."

"Why did they take him out?"

There was a long pause. Williamson stared at the pictures as if saying a final farewell. "I only know what I've heard."

Black knew that was bullshit. Suit or no suit, this guy still knew what was going down – and usually before it happened. Anything he said was gospel.

"Some say he was working under cover. For MI5."

16

LONDONDERRY, THAT EVENING

Black gazed down at the city in the evening haze. His eye ran over the crazy jumble of buildings stacked along the slowly-turning river. The skyline reached up to the sky in three places: the spires of the two cathedrals, glowering at each other like old adversaries on the two facing hills, and between them, the 19th-century pile that once had been his school.

He picked out the College's green minaret. He turned to Maria Gandelli.

"Two hundred years of conflict in those streets. And there, rising out of it, the only school in the world to produce two Nobel prizewinners," he said.

"Enmity and glory. Two sides of the same coin," said de Vries.

The ghosts in the school belltower, if they were looking up, could have picked out the figures of Black, Gandelli and de Vries on the windlashed hillside of the City Cemetary.

They were gathered at a plain gravestone standing alone, to one side of the main plot. With his wealth, Tom Black could have given his mother a marble mausoleum. But her modesty in life decreed a simple stone in death.

Gandelli read the inscription:

> 'Mary Elisabeth Black
> 1924-1977
> *Until we meet again*'

"The odd phrase at the bottom was her personal request," said Black. "Something or other from the latin."

Gandelli pulled her coat collar tighter around her chin. "No, it's from father. It's from the Italian. *Ci incontreremo ancora*. It is the Gandelli family motto."

Behind them, a stocky figure in a black overcoat and trilby hat entered the cemetary through the side gate. Black watched him, a black outline against the sky, as he walked along the main drive that traversed the graveyard from right to left.

The man turned into one of the side paths that led him into the untidy clutter of the graves.

He knelt before a white marble stone, and began picking leaves and windblown ribbons off the sparsely-covered plot. He stuffed the debris into a plastic bag, tucked it away into his pocket, and crossed himself.

Black looked at de Vries. "Do you feel it?" He nodded towards the kneeling man. "We'll imagine every innocent passer-by to be the killer they have sent after us. Every one. Until we get them."

Below them, in the city, a clutch of starlings swirled up between the cathedrals, peppering the sky. Black felt the first drops of a light rain.

*****

Black looked around the interior of the Grand Central Bar, where they had taken refuge from the rain.

Maria Gandelli was agitated. Black was still insisting they could locate their pursuers by 'conventional' means. But conventional means would take time, and time was what they didn't have.

"You have got to pull in all your favours. Even from this Williamson. We have no more time."

"She's right, Tom," said de Vries. "If these guys are as good as you think, we're not going to see them coming."

"Talking to Williamson was one thing. Asking him to send out his dogs is another. If you'd been around here in the 70s, you would know. Those guys make the mafia look like kids in a playground."

At Stormont, Black had run some checks on Williamson's grouping within the movement.

"Williamson's boys found an informer in their ranks in September 1973. Later that winter, they found the guy's body on the Ards Peninsula. All over the Ards Peninsula. If we bring Williamson in, he will wreak havoc. It would draw attention to us."

Black was thinking that Gandelli had a lot to learn about the war in Ireland. It was a long way from the glitzy catwalks of Milan, and the tranquility of Portofino.

"So what next?" she said, sipping the hot port Black had set before her.

"We make unofficial use of official channels. I'll talk to my contact tonight. What about Foley?"

Now it was de Vries' turn to be adamant. "Keep Foley out of it. He talks to London. That's like talking directly to MI5. Besides, Special Branch are probably listening on the line – and not to monitor customer satisfaction, either."

The strain of the last days was showing on Black's brow. He rubbed the back of his neck.

The surly barman was standing where Mary Black had once bustled back and forth, between the beertaps and the antique mirror, absentmindedly wiping pint glasses. The brass rail along the front, where Joe Gandelli, Moose, and Telesco had stood, had dulled a little over the decades.

The barman scrutinised Tom Black, but with no flicker of recognition for the figure often seen emerging from the Dail or No.10.

His eyes wandered to the long legs of Maria Gandelli. He wondered if she was a hooker. The jewellery and fabrics should have told him that she was not.

"This is the room where Joe Gandelli first met Mary Black. Would they have believed that, fifty years later, an Italian assassin would be toasting them in the company of an old soldier from the French colonies, and an Irish..."

Black paused, choosing the right word to describe himself.

Gandelli finished his sentence for him.

"...an Irish patriot."

*****

ARDSALLAGH

Maria Gandelli had an eye for fine bone china.

Otherwise, she would have hammered the Belleek teacup down

more violently than she did, before storming out of the kitchen. Tom Black was red-faced with frustration.

"She's a viper," he said to de Vries. "The woman is obsessed with killing."

De Vries shifted in his chair. Yet again, Gandelli was pushing Black to pull out all the stops. This time, she wanted to put the frights on Quila, to get the name of the contractors on their tail. De Vries wasn't going to take sides in an argument between brother and sister. Especially when both could handle a gun.

"Tom, it won't take them long to realise you are still alive. Maria knows how these people think. They will come after us again. And she's right: with the contacts, a hit can be organised quickly. Contract offered, vendor secured, half a million downpayment made. The whole thing tied up in a couple of days."

The door opened. A now-calm Maria Gandelli stepped back to her chair.

Maria looked sheepishly at Black. It was as close as her ego would let her come to an apology.

"What did Quila say on the phone?"

"She said all she could say, on an open phone line. That there were 'sensitivities' she couldn't talk about. People she would compromise if she gave us the documents on the group that's behind this."

On Gandelli's neck, the hackles rose again. Black had to come around to her way of thinking. And quickly. "Look, Tom, she's our only hope. We have to pressure her. We can't do without her, if we are to get out of this in one piece."

De Vries peered up from under his eyebrows. "And presumably you think letting her discuss it with the barrel of your Beretta will ... ease things along?"

The glance she fired told him he had gone too far. Black stepped in to stop the volcano erupting again.

"Look, I've asked Foley for the chopper, it will be here in the morning at six. We'll be at Quila's home by eight."

Gandelli had to have the last word. "She has to be forced to co-operate. We have no time to deal with bureaucratic red tape."

"Maria," said Black, looking at his watch, "just leave the Beretta in its case, ok?"

*****

LONDON, THAT MORNING

Sir Anthony Cathcart slammed down the lid of his laptop and snatched up the yellow phone on his office desk.

"Geraint. Still no report of a murder in the Irish Republic. I checked the Irish wire services as well."

"They won't report a murder, Anthony. It will be a disappearance. I gave instructions that our agent is to dispose of the body. Forgive me if I neglected to mention it. It would gain us a little time."

It was only eleven, but Cathcart's nerves were failing him. He had already had his first single malt of the day.

"Geraint, something's wrong. Let us suppose our vendor has been eliminated by Black, or Black has gone to ground. Our anonymity could be at risk."

"Agreed. I suggest putting all matters on hold. Pending clarity on Mister Black," said Welles.

"Should we convene Prometheus?"

"There would be no point. Our mandate from the group to move on Black is already in place. The method is of little consequence, even if it means switching to an alternative plan."

"And do we have an alternative plan?" said Cathcart.

"Anthony, sorry again for keeping you in the dark, but there is a 'reserve strategy' I've dreamed up. I didn't think it would be needed. But it's imperative that we conclude this matter – eliminate Black, that is – before the summit at the weekend."

Cathcart was irritated. This was the first he had heard of any reserve strategy. Welles was treating him like an office junior. The strain showed in his voice as he continued.

"What, Geraint, have you 'dreamed up'?"

"I have a second agent already in place. A local operator. Someone who has helped us out in Ireland in the past. He knows the usual 'modus operandi' of these terror groups. He was particularly good at making his work look like an 'internal feud' scenario. It should look like Black was killed by one of the Irish groupings."

"Geraint, my gut feeling is that vendor A is either dead or has failed. I would suggest that we deploy your man forthwith."

Welles heaved a sigh of relief at Cathcart's agreement.

He had already despatched vendor B, ninety minutes ago.

*****

The darkest hour is just before dawn.

De Vries thought of the proverb as he stared at the heavy silhouettes of the trees around the house. It was 5am.

They had snatched four hours of sleep before Black had been wakened by a call from Heneghan. The chopper was on schedule, and would be landing in an hour.

Gandelli was seated sideways at the table, her shoulder towards Black. Between them sat two bowls of steaming coffee, a butter dish with a yellow flower, and a breadboard stacked high with Mary Gallagher's wheaten bread.

The bread was untouched. A silence as hard as the butts of a stone wall filled the room. Black had not caved in. He was determined that the 'softly, softly' approach was still the way to go.

"Again: there is no alternative but to force the issue. We cannot waste valuable minutes with polite 'requests' to this Quila woman," said Gandelli. She looked sullen. She had not slept well.

"Masterful understatement, Maria," responded Black. "'Force the issue' is a pleasant word for a very unpleasant way forward."

"This does not concern only you," said Gandelli. "I have broken a contract. I am not a car dealer, Tom. I am a hired killer. I cannot simply return their deposit. None of us is safe, until this group is out of action. If we fail to locate them, it's a bullet for you, and a lifetime on the run for me."

Her bleak scenario was making de Vries uncomfortable. "I have a few things to gather up, before we go." Dark-faced, he lifted the car keys and his coffee, went into the hall, and climbed the stairs.

In his bedroom, de Vries knelt on the floor. From beneath the bed he withdrew a battered brown leather suitcase with frayed buckle-straps. A present from his father. Chiselled in the leather, the initials JdV.

He lifted the lid, and slid his hand into a special pocket at the rear of the case. He held up a scaly-looking cockerel's foot, with three toenails like an old woman's fingers. Around the ankle of the luck charm, a purple ribbon was tied in an ornate bow.

He pushed his hand under the neat stack of shirts a second time, and produced a small blue carton of .22mm bullets. *Voodoo is fine. A little earthly insurance is better still.*

Damn. On the windowpane he could see the driving rain, and his revolver was in the glove compartment in the jeep. He pulled on his jacket.

He was thinking of Schanz and Adamsen, of the Legion camp in Chad. He was thinking how, for twenty years now, he had owed his life to Black.

Maybe this would be his chance to repay the debt.

*****

At ten minutes to six, Captain Brendan O'Malley guided the Sikorsky past Milford on its west side, and peered to his right to search for moonlight on Mulroy Bay, and the irregular shape of Bunlin Bridge.

In the passenger seat, Matt Heneghan cursed the weather-god that brought rain nine months of the year to Donegal.

First came the flash. Then a puffball of orange fire that sent the bonnet of the Chrysler spinning upwards, until it was thirty feet over the ground.

It looked like slow motion. The twisted sheet of metal reached its apex as the boom of the blast reached the chopper. It began its long cascade back to the ground, lit from beneath by the still-bursting fireball that flooded the façade of the house with an eerie light.

O'Malley pulled the Sikorsky to port, fighting to make sense of what was happening. Heneghan had thrown himself over to the starboard window and could already see the flipped-over chassis of the jeep rocking on the driveway, like a spinning top at the end of its spin. The flames glowed through a confetti shower of glass, gravel and dirt.

In the house, Black and Gandelli had thrown themselves to the ground. Gandelli held her right hand over a gaping cut on her temple, and waved with her left to indicate she was all right.

Black stumbled to his feet, and grabbed his pistol from the worktop. Snapping back the safety catch, he ran up the steps into the hall. The lights in the house were gone, but the hall was filled with yellow light from the blazing jeep outside.

He half-tripped on a heavy obstacle on the ground. One of the door panels had blown in, on to the floor. The other half of the entrance door hung from a hinge, jammed under the beam of the collapsing jamb.

The smoke billowing up from the jeep had turned black as the tyres began melting in the heat. The drive was a ten-feet-wide crater that seemed to tremble before Black's eyes.

The crackling of the flames was drowned out by the drumbeat of the chopper, as it circled overhead.

*****

"I'll take care of the Gardaí when they get here," said Heneghan, pushing Gandelli and Black towards the idling chopper. "This was no accident. You have to get out of here."

"De Vries," said Black, staring over his shoulder. "De Vries."

Heneghan could see confusion and shock in his eyes. "De Vries was in the jeep," he said to Black, pushing their travel bags on to the floor of the Sikorsky's cabin. Nothing more needed to be said.

"I'll tell the press we can't identify the body. Or bodies. That will give you more time," he called, as Gandelli and Black strapped themselves into their seats. He slammed the door of the chopper, and ran back towards the still-blazing truck.

Black placed something on the bag at Gandelli's feet. "I just found this on the ground." It was the cockerel's foot, the ribbon charred from the blast.

Gandelli pressed the dressing that was stanching the flow of blood from her forehead. Both looked back at the hull of the jeep. The sour smell of diesel soaked into their throats.

O'Malley pressed the throttle and pulled them up out of the chaos, away into the air.

In the kitchen, Heneghan searched for the phone to get Foley. Porcelain from the breakfast table was strewn everywhere.

In the chopper, Black looked at Gandelli. Both had the same thought. *A bomb has a way of changing your point of view.*

Far below, the blue lights of the first squad cars were speeding down the hill from Milford.

"Ok, Maria," said Black, as the Sikorsky tacked to the south.

"We do it your way. We're going to get these bastards. It's time to 'force the issue' now."

*****

The car swept quickly out of Baldonnel Aerodrome, ten miles south-west of Dublin.

Heneghan had phoned to say he had informed Foley of the death of de Vries. The clock was running. Black used the one-hour drive to Evelyn de Burca's house to unleash the hounds.

A call to Jimmy Williamson set up an interrogation of Deano, to identify the group behind the Danieli contract. This time, no request to keep the enquiries low-key. Black did not care.

Now he had to tell de Burca to forget her worries about 'sensitivities'. Hesitation was no longer an option.

Maria Gandelli looked out at the lush green quilt of countryside speeding by. She was in Ireland, where she never thought she'd be, with a half-brother she never knew she had, and an assassin on her tail. A lot had changed in a week.

For the first time, she knew how it felt to be hunted. A far cry from standing at the safe end of the gun. She had put herself in the firing line for a man she hardly knew. It had cost her a quarter of a million, and if Quila or Evelyn or whatever her name was couldn't or wouldn't play ball, she could be looking over her shoulder for the rest of her life.

The tables had turned. The predator had become the prey.

*****

"I'll go in alone," said Black, as the Mercedes glided to a soft stop in front of the manse where Evelyn de Burca lived.

Despite the early hour, she was not surprised to see him. However, she knew nothing of the jeep bomb. He would not mention it immediately.

"Evelyn, I now believe there is real substance to your information about a contract killer. Our only hope is to trace the contractor. I reckon we have a few days only."

De Burca was sitting motionless, listening, the light from the fire flickering on her face.

"Tom, that would present me with ... extreme difficulty. You know that sometimes we receive information indirectly ... what I mean to say is, information we don't officially have. If it came out that this came from Foreign Affairs or even from myself privately, it would seriously compromise..."

De Burca trailed off and sighed, shaking her head. "It would be the end of the line, certainly for me, probably for Foley as well, not to mention our contact, who is still very much 'live'. I was hoping you could have identified them through your contacts in France. I'm afraid that giving you our information is ... out of the question."

De Burca visibly shuddered as Black shouted, incandescent with rage. "Evelyn, my friend Jacques de Vries is dead. They bombed my car last night – at my own bloody house. At Ardsallagh."

Black stopped, turned, walked to the window that faced on to the rose garden. He composed himself.

"Evelyn, they're not just out for a target in London, they're out for me as well. Maybe it's political, maybe it's because they know I'm on to them. But if they know about me, they may know about you. That means you are *already* compromised."

De Burca's face had turned as stern as the stone fireplace beside her. She had got the message.

"I can't go back to Ardsallagh, not with a contract killer waiting in the woods. And if you can't help me, then let's say our goodbyes now, for one or both of us will be dead within the week."

De Burca stood up. She looked like a heavy weight had been loaded on to her shoulders.

She took a deep breath.

"There is a secret grouping in Whitehall which calls itself Prometheus. No point in even asking Foley's department – we hardly know about it ourselves. It has just a handful of members, but all 'high-ups'. They work as a kind of 'star chamber' – taking unoffical action behind the scenes, with their own agenda, that sort of thing."

De Burca paced to the far end of the room. For the first time, Black heard the tock-tock of the large grandfather clock in the corner. He had started to notice the ticking of clocks. Seconds had become important.

"There are seven in the core group, for a long time we've known the identities of the top three. There is also 'Member 8'. Someone who does not meet with them, someone so senior that their identity is known only to two of the others."

Black would have looked surprised, if he were not so stressed already. "So senior? You mean someone at the Palace? Or Downing Street?"

"It has to be. Someone white-hot. Someone whose discovery would bring down a government," said de Burca.

She opened the door to her study. "I'll get you the file."

Twenty minutes later, Black opened the door of the Mercedes.

Gandelli was painting her nails. In the top of her handbag he saw a compact, a bottle of Chanel, and the grey handle of a pistol.

"Maria, you gave me your word. You said you'd leave the Beretta behind."

"No. I said I would not use it. That's a different thing." She paused for a second as she topped up her lipstick. "If your friend in there hadn't wanted to help, well, a Beretta and a stern word are better than a stern word alone. Besides, you agreed. From now on, we do it my way."

Black was careful to ensure she saw the folder in his hand. "Force was never going to be necessary. Not with Evelyn. As I said before – we go back a long way."

"So." Gandelli strained to widen her eyes as she produced the mascara brush. "She has put her career on the line for an old friend."

"I explained the gravity of the situation."

"So she is reasonable, after all."

She turned away from her make-up mirror for a second to look at Black. He saw the glint of mischief in her eye.

"Or was it the action of a woman who cares?"

As the car pulled away from the house, Black looked out at the carefully-groomed hedges. He was searching for the correct phrase.

"It was ... it was a long time ago."

17

MUNICH, THE NEXT DAY

Jürgen Karmann was reading his horoscope as he trotted up the marble staircase leading to his office at 'Die Zeitung' newspaper.

'Taurus. Even the best-laid plans will not come to fruition today. Better not to plan at all. Today's motto is: 'play it by ear'.'

Sounds just like any other day, he muttered to himself, and pushed open the grey door marked 'Editorial'. As he entered the newsroom, the frantic energy of a news organisation running at full speed swept over him.

His desk sat under a heap of papers in the corner of the second floor, looking down on the fashionable clutter of Hohenzollernstrasse, a tree-lined thoroughfare in the Schwabing quarter.

Outside, a light rain was turning the falling leaves to a brown mulch. He frowned at the drabness of the view as he poured the coffee dregs from his permacup into the rubber plant on the window sill. Like him, the plant survived on sunlight and caffeine. He crossed the newsroom to the percolator, to fetch the next one.

Herzog, his editor, was topping up his cup as Karmann approached. "I took a call for you this morning, from Tom Black, the Irish guy from *Fondation Noir*. He said expect a disk, and it's important. He wants you to ring him when you get it."

Herzog had the world-weary look of those career journalists who haven't seen the sun in thirty years. He had lost count of how many ashtrays he'd worn out over the decades, and his complexion was the same milky grey as the computer on his desk.

"It wasn't in my mail."

"Before you ask, he wouldn't say what it was. I hope you're not going to get caught in that porn cinema in Feilitzstrasse again, looking for envelopes under seats." Herzog was wearing his sarcastic smile.

Karmann cringed at the memory. He had been retrieving a dossier of leaked documents, left in the fifth row by his 'deep throat' contact at the Finance Ministry. The manager had called security. *We have another carpet crawler in there.* They had escorted him from the cinema.

Karmann took the hot cup back to his corner. The drab landscape of Munich was still outside the window. At the next desk, Inge Schröder was scanning the cover stories in the morning press.

"Jesus," she said in her distinctive Berlin accent. "Over a hundred wars going on around the globe, and all we're worried about is whether the Bundeskanzler dyes his hair."

"That's an easy one," smiled Karmann, his eyes narrowing as he sipped from his cup. "He's a politician. If he says yes, he doesn't. If he says no, he probably does."

Schröder smiled back. She had joined the paper a week before. There was chemistry between her and Karmann, though no sparks as yet. But then, it was still only ten o'clock.

"Oh, just in for you." She tossed a red and grey courier envelope across to him. Bending backwards, he caught it with his free hand.

Karmann loaded up the cd-rom and flicked through the xerox sheets and grainy black-and-white photographs in the folder. The rain continued to run down the window pane beside him.

For the first time in months, he let a fresh coffee go cold.

He picked up the documents, walked into Herzog's office, and closed the door.

*****

Rain was also falling outside the window of room 217 of the St. Stephen's, a small hotel in a secluded street in the Dublin suburb of Rathgar.

Black and Gandelli had taken adjoining rooms at the back of the shabby Georgian house, overlooking a row of similar 4-storey town houses fronted with cascading steps and well-tended urban gardens.

The view of a doctor's surgery, a solicitor's office and an interior design studio was comforting. It made Black feel safe as he leaned at the window, taking in the fresh air.

The rustling of the trees was broken by the robotic sing-song of his mobile phone. On the fascia display he recognised the number of Jimmy Williamson.

"We got hold of Deano. He said he knew nothing about MI5, or who had ordered their trip to Venice. I believed him. In the end."

Then it clicked. Black recalled the news report he had heard two hours earlier.

"A 27-year-old man was found this morning on waste ground in Belfast's Ardoyne. He was nailed to a wooden fence through the hands, and had a thorn branch tied around his head. Police are treating the incident as a punishment beating. The man remains in a stable condition in hospital..."

"Jimmy, is that the mock crucifixion they mentioned on the radio?"

Black heard Williamson snigger. "We like to think we took our inspiration from Venice, Tom. The Italian renaissance and all that.

"An interrogation doesn't have to be a totally negative experience."

*****

On Milan's *Corso Vittorio Emanuelle*, a street performer masquerading as a gold statue slowly turned his head to face the tourist throng on the *Piazza del Duomo*.

A tall, dapper and very agitated man in a beige corduroy suit was blustering up from the cathedral square, barking into his cellphone as he went. He was flapping his free arm in a very Italian way. A group of tame pigeons hopped lazily aside as he passed.

He was Raymondo Getto, deputy artistic director of the Fashion House Gandelli SpA, and co-ordinator of the Maria Gandelli Spring Collection 2005. And he was apoplectic with rage as he harangued his assistant, Giorgio Cambolo, who was four hundred yards away, in the Gandelli headquarters further down the street.

"Buying tweeds in Ireland? I don't care how hard she is to reach. The Fashion Week is five weeks away and we still have four designs to finalise. Get her now. Get her back here by Monday – but get her!"

*****

Jürgen Karmann shivered as he pulled the payphone door closed behind him, and stared bleakly across the rainwashed cobbles of Hohenzollernplatz.

A row of forlorn-looking green plastic tables lined the front of the Adler-Café, each mottled with bubbles where the rain had collected.

Across the square, a couple of bums were drinking cans of import beer at the door of a liquor store. There was nobody else in sight.

He sat Black's folder on the shelf beside him, and pushed his callcard into the slot.

"Tom. It's Karmann. I just spoke to Herzog about your package. No, he won't touch it. Not unless this woman Ellingham will go on the record. It would be too hot. If you can get her, let me know and I'll go to him again. Sorry."

Karmann slammed the door behind him and half-jogged the hundred metres back to the office door. He had no folder under his arm. It was still on the payphone shelf.

*****

LONDON, NEXT MORNING, 11AM

Gandelli pulled round the wheel of the hired Voyager and took them off the exit roundabout at Stansted Airport, heading for the city.

Black was on the phone to Stephen Sloane, an Irish-born political editor at one of the more respected editorial offices on Fleet Street.

Sloane's 16-year-old brother had been killed by a British jeep on a Belfast street in 1981. A junior minister had spoken on tv news that night, announcing that 'traffic accidents are, unfortunately, a real danger in a riot situation'. It had hardened Sloane's cynical view of Whitehall, whom he suspected of arranging the whitewash.

After Karmann's refusal, Black would have to fight the battle on home turf, despite the extra risk. And Sloane was the best contact he had.

By 11.30am, the rush hour should have been past. Black recalled some half-forgotten line about a 'city that never sleeps'. A sea of slow-moving traffic nosed through a thicket of red and white cones and long strips of plastic tape. They were stuck in construction-land,

and Sloane would be waiting in The Cheshire Cheese at noon.

"Pull over. I'll take the tube. We can meet up at the hotel later."

As the train rolled into the tunnel that would take it underground, Black stared at the faces of the commuters, rolling left and right like a sullen, silent choir. This, he thought, is how a sheep feels on its way to the shambles.

"You were dead right to try to go abroad," said Sloane, once Black had brought two frothing pints of red ale. The wooden floor of Fleet Street's famous pub ensured a cacophony of clattering feet. They could talk freely, with no fear of being overheard.

"Whitehall would attempt a total cover-up. Scotland Yard would go along, pressure would be put on the tv people. There had been rumours from time to time over the years of some kind of secret society inside MI5. If this Prometheus Group knows you're on to them, we haven't got much time."

Sloane had not batted an eyelid when Black had told him about De Vries.

Black fingered the cockerel's foot at the bottom of his pocket.

"But Karmann in Munich was right," said Sloane.

"We still need this woman on the inside. If there's a shred of doubt, Whitehall will react with a blanket denial, followed by a smoke-screen."

"I can try to get Ellingham. We have one slender hope: part of her wants to talk. That's a start," said Black.

Sloane rose to go. "I'll write it up and hold off while you try to reach her. I can keep space in tomorrow's edition until 9pm.

"But without her, it's no-go, Tom. Dead in the water. And so are you."

*****

The anonymity of the metropolis, which he had otherwise so hated, was a comfort to Black now.

He felt safe weaving through the maelstrom of red buses and courier vans that slid, in fits and starts, from Green Park up to Piccadilly.

Gandelli was waiting for him in the entrance lounge of the hotel. For a woman with a price on her head, she was looking remarkably unruffled, one long leg crossed over the other, leafing through a copy of 'Harper's Bazaar'. She had finished her glass of café latte.

Black sat down, and brought her up to date. "I talked again to Quila. She'll try to contact Ellingham and tell her to be at her London flat at 6pm. She said she'll keep it vague as to why."

"And Ellingham will trust her?"

Black looked out the window at the bustling street. To a dead man, the bristling energy of a metropolis holds a compelling fascination.

He did not answer her. He had no answer to give.

*****

LONDON 5.30PM

Dusk was falling as Black pulled the land cruiser over in front of a long row of town houses in a leafy road in Pimlico.

Number twenty-six was a typical urban dwelling, with mullioned windows and quaint greenery peering down at the street from the upper floors.

It could have been the house of a schoolteacher, or a postmistress. It was the house of Simone Ellingham, middle-ranking executive at MI6, and one of the jury that had ordered Black's execution.

The photo of Ellingham in the dossier was several years old. He hoped he would recognise her when she arrived. He turned up the car heater, and settled down to wait.

In the end, the nondescript woman in the neat blue trouser suit who emerged from the silver Lexus could have been a schoolteacher after all.

As she entered the small front garden, closing the gate behind her, Black jogged across the road.

"I am Tom Black".

Her shoulders jerked visibly and her car keys fell to the ground, before she looked around. She tensed herself, and regained her composure, before she spoke.

The man standing at the gate had a dignified bearing that told her instantly she was in no danger. It was just as well; she had left her firearm in the office. Again.

"We had best talk inside," she said, stooping to retrieve the bundle of keys.

Black mounted the four broad steps. Two large barrels of

evergreen shrubs stood guard on the doorstep, to the left and the right of a heavy, mock-tudor door.

Ellingham led him into a parlour off the hallway. She turned on a lamp with a tiffany shade that threw a burst of colour into the encroaching darkness, and draped her coat over the chair.

There was no point in wasting time with further small-talk. It was obvious why he was there.

"I know about the plan for a killing in London, and about the contract on me personally. And I know about Prometheus."

He opened the dossier and laid it gently on the coffee table. The photos of herself, Welles, and Cathcart that lay uppermost on the sheaf of papers proved what he was saying, even before she picked up the sheets and scanned the notes.

Ellingham could see that Black had not come to ask her to cancel the contract. That would take care of itself, when the information in the dossier became public.

Black waited until she had looked over each of the pages before continuing.

"You were the one who leaked the information to Evelyn de Burca. To Quila, that is. You know this is the end for Welles, Cathcart and the others. It's the end for you too. Why did you do it? Because of the royal?"

Black was calling her bluff. His notion that the other contract was for a royal was a hunch more than a certainty.

Simone Ellingham was pensive. She too knew it was over.

"No, Mr. Black. It wasn't just that. And it really doesn't matter which 'royal', before you ask. Put it down to something I saw in my father. He too was in the service, but he had no part in this sort of 'covert operation'. In the end, it was goings-on of this kind that got to him. His conscience forced him out."

Morality. Conscience. Now, Black could see her weakness. Her Achilles' heel.

"Maybe, Miss Ellingham, this is your last chance to purge yourself. To do the right thing. To feel clean."

"I'm not sure that anything could make me feel clean any more. I assume you intend to publish a copy of this dossier. When will that be?"

"It has probably happened already. And part of you wants to help me. I have a journalist at one of the papers. Will you speak to him?"

Ellingham shook her head. "There's no point. You know how it works. They ... we ... do a fine job on covering up this sort of thing. You have information here, photos. But proof? I don't see anything I would call proof."

"If you want to stop the murder of the royal, you will have to talk," said Black.

Ellingham's tone was plain and even. Matter-of-fact. She could have been talking to an old friend. "Prometheus will not proceed with that now. As for the contract on you, that will also be terminated. I would imagine you have nothing to fear. But go on the record to substantiate this ... speculative dossier? No. I think not. This is the end of our little chat, Mr. Black. Good evening."

*****

Black fired the jeep into life and drove for all of thirty seconds, parking in an identical leafy street around the corner.

It was 6.57pm. He dialled Sloane's number at the paper.

As the phone rang, he unhooked the tape recorder in his inside pocket from the wire microphone that ran down inside his sleeve, and was clipped to his wristwatch.

He flicked the switch to rewind.

"Stephen. You were right to give me the tape recorder. She wasn't prepared to talk to you. She's confirmed the royal, and mentioned Prometheus by name. I'll bring it right over.

"Run the story!"

*****

MI5 OFFICES, FRIDAY AFTERNOON

Stanley Newell liked Fridays.

Fridays suited him. On Fridays, most of the spooks on the 5th floor of the MI5 offices on London's Embankment were gone by four o'clock, motoring up to country retreats in Buckinghamshire or Cambridgeshire, or walking to the warm, companionable pubs around Piccadilly to usher in the weekend over an early evening drink.

This made it easier for Stanley, hygiene operative with Sterilite

Office Services, to clean their terminals and phones. The photocopiers were still. He had peace and quiet.

At 4.24pm, one lone secretary was left at her PC, finishing off a draft of something or other before following the rest of them into the weekend.

When the woman screamed, it shattered the tranquility of Stanley's entire day. When she screamed, and screamed, and would not stop screaming, Stanley wondered if they had a mouse in the office. With an irritated sigh, he laid his chamois and sterile wipes on the desk, and followed the sound around the corner to where she was standing, in front of an open office door.

Sir Anthony Cathcart's brains were spread over the large gilt-framed mirror that filled the wall behind his 18th-century rosewood desk. A copy of the morning's *Telegraph* was open before him.

The pistol and silencer had fallen on to the newspaper, beside the phone.

At that moment, three miles away, Sir Geraint Welles was being led in handcuffs from his club by three detectives from Scotland Yard.

Stanley looked at the phone. It was the BT Paragon 500. Stanley had always thought of the 500 as a nice piece of technology.

Now it's sleek curves were spattered with Sir Anthony Cathcart's blood, and Stanley would have to clean it.

It had really ruined his Friday.

18

Lake Garda, Italy, two weeks later

Seagulls were crying over the lakefront at Desenzano as the two figures walked slowly under the black fingers of the mangrove trees along the water's edge.

Joe Gandelli carried his father's hazel stick in his left hand. It complemented the linen suit in rich burgundy, which he wore with a silk handkerchief in the breast pocket. In place of a tie, he wore a silk cravate designed by his daughter, engraved with the small black bird, the crest of the House of Gandelli.

Tom Black had come to Italy the previous day.

Drawing the collar of his overcoat tightly under his chin, he marvelled at his father's robust constitution.

The awkwardness of their first meeting had given way to an easy confidence. They had liked each other instantly. For Black, the curious events of the last month had brought a new dimension, given him an anchor.

Gandelli, too, was assimilating the changes, just when he had thought life had no more twists and turns ahead.

They had talked. It was a time for reflection. A time to reassess.

Joe Gandelli had seen more in his first forty years than most men see in seventy-five. But it was twenty years after 'Pearl', as he called it, before he had begun *noticing*.

With growing maturity and less fire in his belly, things had begun to reveal a deeper resonance. He told Tom that he had been forty-five years of age, before he had fully freed himself from the uncertainties of youth.

That was forty years ago. Nowadays, only fond recollections

remained, he said. He had banished old enmities, like pressing poison out of a rotten wound. Now, he was content.

"If death were to come today, I am ready," he had said.

Pearl Harbor had been the turning point in his life. It had thrown fame around him like a cloak. The cloak had given protection from the elements, brought financial security. But, he said, only with the birth of Maria had he found true happiness.

Maria had left them alone, she had enough to do in Milan. She had pressed Tom's arm and told him he would have 'a private hour' with his father, as if some hourglass had been turned over that would soon run out of sand. But even with Joe in his eighty-eighth year, both men felt that they had time. This day was a beginning.

In two weeks they would attend the launch of the Maria Gandelli 'Collezione Nuove' at the Intercontinental. Joseph – as they called him in her office – disliked the glitz of it all. The controlled hysteria smacked of a 1950s American tv game show. He explained to Tom that he attended for the sake of Maria, sat away from the front rows, read the catalogue in the light of flickering flashbulbs and listened to the glitterati with their exaggerated enthusiasm. He had long ago lost interest in the mannequins, who were half his daughter's age. He was no longer burdened with the languid sexuality of younger men, and found the girls scrawny and ridiculous.

"I tell Maria they are her peacocks. I must sound like an aging vicar. *Il diavolo, quando è vecchio, si fa frate.* When the devil grows old, Tom, he becomes a monk." Both men smiled.

In his inner pocket, Black touched the rough manila envelope he had dug out of the old chocolate box where he kept his personal effects. It was a letter his mother had written to him when she was forty-eight.

In the letter she had referred to his father as 'an honest, decent man'. That was to be Tom Black's gift to Joe Gandelli. He would give it to him later.

Joe had mentioned Mary Black in passing. She had been brought into the conversation once, and then put away.

"I had no choice, you know. They ordered me back to the US. Heroism is built on high ideals. Perhaps on hero-worship. It is a thing for boys. As you grow into adulthood, the generals take you out of the line of fire, before you begin to see through them. Before you begin to ask questions."

Tom seemed to understand.

Black was thinking of the Legion, of an old comrade, Zellner the Belgian, who, still a soldier at thirty-eight, had been punchdrunk, useless for civilian life.

"So you have lost your heroes now?" He asked his father.

Gandelli shook his head, looked at the water. "They've become a little more human, perhaps. But I can still admire them."

They watched a single raven soaring along the water's edge, and listened to the music of the lake.